Lawless Guns

Imprisoned for murder, innocent Luther Larkin feels only resentment towards the town of Black Bear Crossing and its lawman. But when an unexpected confession sets Luther free he finds himself drawn back to his boyhood home, and pretty soon trouble, in the form of Marcus Cooper, a neighbouring rancher, seeks him out.

But Luther is determined to prove to the town that he is no longer a kid to be pushed around. And he isn't the only one who has been drawn back to Black Bear Crossing: deranged killer Donald Ricket has a score to settle with the town, and only Luther stands between him and his goal.

Lawless Guns

M. Duggan

A Black Horse Western

ROBERT HALE · LONDON

ISBN 978-0-7198-0577-6

Robert Hale Limited
Clerkenwell House
Clerkenwell Green
London EC1R 0HT

www.halebooks.com

Typeset by
Derek Doyle & Associates, Shaw Heath
Printed and bound in Great Britain by
CPI Antony Rowe, Chippenham and Eastbourne

CHAPTER ONE

Luther Larkin had killed a man: his first. He had often wondered how it would feel to take a life. Well now he knew and he hadn't felt anything at all. This was not surprising. He'd been too long inside the hell that was the state penitentiary.

This was not the first time a man had been murdered inside the prison, nor would it be the last.

'Well,' he said, 'Seems I can do what needs to be done.' He was speaking to his cellmate: Ambrose Penrose convicted killer.

The brutish face of a guard appeared at the grille. 'Be on your best behaviour,' he warned.

The friendly smile did not slip from Penrose's round face. Luther wasn't fooled. He believed that one day pretty soon Warden Comfrey would pay for the indignity he had heaped upon Ambrose Penrose. He exhibited the man as he might an animal in a zoo or a lunatic in a place Penrose referred to as Bedlam.

Comfrey had soon discovered that women, respectable or otherwise, seemed unnaturally fascinated with the notorious killer and would pay handsomely just to catch a glimpse of the man. They were all welcome, although Comfrey was careful to keep the two types of women, respectable and disreputable, separate.

Respectable ones came morning, the disreputable late afternoon. As it was afternoon they knew which type to expect.

Luther dropped to his knees and began to pray. And Penrose, facing the wall began to knock his forehead against it. It was expected that they would put on some kind of a show. Penrose was always careful not to damage himself.

'Well, here they are,' the guard announced. 'Just take a look, then move along quickly. I ain't got all day to pander to you ladies!'

A gloved hand dropped a note on the floor. 'I'm from your home town, Luke Larkin. Walt Grainger sends his regards.' Then she was gone, but not before Luther had picked up the missive.

'Well, now you have seen them!' the guard observed. 'Lunatics both,' he continued cheerfully to inform the women. 'Now come on, you've had your money's worth. Get on out of here, you no-account floozies.'

Once the guard had left Luther read the missive. He was kind of surprised.

'I'm sorry. I've done you a wrong. I'm confessing to the killing,' Walt had written. He then went on to say that he was a dying man and needed to make his peace with the Lord.

'What the hell this is about I cannot say,' Luther handed the note to Penrose. 'Think anyone will believe Walt's confession?' he asked doubtfully.

'They sure will. A deathbed confession always goes down well,' Penrose observed grimly. 'Let us hope you are around long enough to see the conclusion of our plans.'

'Oh, I'll be around long enough to see you out of here,' Luther retorted. 'You have my word on that!'

Both men knew that Comfrey the warden had ordered extra vigilance. Embezzler Silas Wright had snitched. But Wright had not known much. And before Wright could ferret out the details he had been dealt with. The man had been a damn fool. He'd been trying to curry favour with Comfrey and had lost his life as a result.

'We must make our move sooner rather than later,' Penrose advised.

Luther nodded. 'We have just one more key to make!' He grinned. 'And I have made the impression.' He tore the letter into small pieces, placed them in his mouth and swallowed them. 'I'm putting Walt Grainger and his damn fool confession out of my mind.'

'Damn fool?' Penrose queried.

'That's right. I know I did not murder Hamish Cooper and I am pretty damn sure Grainger is not the murderer. But in any event I'm putting the events that occurred in Black Bear Crossing out of my head for now.'

Overloading the mind, he knew, drove many an inmate crazy. Once or twice he felt he'd come close to madness himself. But given his circumstances this was not surprising. He smiled grimly, wondering what hand fate would deal next.

He came to a decision.

'Penrose.'

'What?'

'If things don't work out and we can't get out of this damn hell-hole you are to do me a great favour!'

'Which is?'

'I'd like you to snap my neck.'

'That ain't a problem.' Someone else might have tried to talk him out of the idea but not Penrose. 'But surely, Luther, you are man enough to slit your own throat if needs be. There is always a way out one way or another.'

Luther considered the words. 'Trouble is,' he at last responded, 'I ain't exactly sure what kind of man I am. I ain't had a chance to find out. I was but a youngster when they shipped me here.'

Penrose chuckled. 'You ain't that young fool any more, that is for sure. You've got patience to see things through. And you're the only man I've ever relied upon.' He paused, 'But don't you fret. We're both on our way out of here.'

Luther nodded. 'I reckon,' he agreed.

With the sun shining in his eyes, Sheriff Amos Standish squinted at the high, forbidding red-stone walls of the penitentiary. Outside the walls a burial was taking place in the prison cemetery.

'Hell, I hope it ain't Luke Larkin.' He urged his horse forward. His two companions followed suit.

'It would make things easier if it were,' Lawyer Robins grumbled.

'Shame on you,' the Reverend Dent chided.

The brutish-looking prison guards eyed the three men with ill-concealed hostility.

'Who are you burying?' the lawman asked without pre-amble, eyeing the cheap coffin.

'Just a no-account bum,' a guard answered with obvious reluctance.

'How did he die?' the lawman asked.

The second guard spat. 'Not natural, that's for sure! One of the mad dogs we house damn near separated his head from his neck; sneaked up on him whilst he was on the latrine and managed to get a wire loop over his head. That's the second one we've lost this way.' He grinned. 'Shocked, are you, lawman? And you, Reverend, you're looking a mite squeamish!'

'Tell me it ain't Luke Larkin,' Standish demanded.

'No, it ain't Larkin!' The guard guffawed. 'We're bursting at the seams here so you could say whoever done it did us a favour!'

'Don't let us keep you men from your business. You're here to see Comfrey!' the older guard interrupted with a warning scowl at his companion, clearly wanting this particular conversation concluded.

'Let's get this over with,' Robins snapped. 'And remember we have nothing to reproach ourselves for. We acted in good faith then and we're acting in good faith now.'

'Indeed we are,' Dent agreed, conveniently forgetting how he had vehemently denounced young Larkin from the pulpit. 'I wonder how he'll be?' Dent mused as they rode through the huge gates. 'But a broken spirit can be mended.' He paused, 'Furthermore, I shall endeavour to make Larkin realize that accepting Rancher Cooper's generous offer will not in the long term be in his best interest. He'll come to grief. He won't know how to handle the money.'

'However, I'm duty bound to inform Larkin of the offer and I believe he'll accept.' Robins smiled patronizingly. 'I will be surprised if he chooses to return to town with us.'

'Fact is we don't know what kind of man we're dealing with!' The lawman shrugged. 'But we'll find out soon enough.'

'One who harbours a grudge, I should imagine,' Robins replied drily. 'He was falsely convicted, after all. You railroaded the boy, Sheriff!'

'The whole town believed him guilty. And so did you. Your defence was a joke.'

'And who would have believed Walter Grainger guilty of such a crime,' the Reverend Dent pacified, thinking the sheriff and the lawyer might come to blows.

From behind his desk Warden Comfrey regarded his visitors with mild blue eyes. He had a friendly face. Behind the warden on the bare, unadorned wall was a large plain cross.

'Do you have the papers?' the warden asked. He took the documents and perused them in silence. Somewhere in the room a fly buzzed annoyingly.

'What kind of man are we dealing with?' Standish enquired.

Comfrey looked up with a satisfied smile upon his face. 'Not a particularly bright man but one who, under my guidance, has found the Lord. You look surprised,' he observed when the lawman's jaw dropped open. This was not the reply that Robin's had expected. 'He's a man who takes pride in his work,' the warden continued.

'His work?' Standish queried.

'Luther is our cleaner,' Comfrey explained.

'Luther?' Standish questioned.

Comfrey nodded. 'Larkin only answers to the name given to him when he was baptized. He says Luke Larkin is long gone!'

'I am surprised he has survived in one piece,' Robins stated bluntly. The silence lengthened. Comfrey did not reply.

'Where is he? Has he been told?' Standish at last demanded.

'He's in his cell. And yes, I informed him myself.'

'And how did he react?' The lawman's tone implied another, unasked, question.

'Have no fear, no threats were uttered. The boy you falsely accused all those years ago has become a man. Luther merely asked that he be allowed time alone in our chapel when the time came for him to leave. I'll have a guard take him to the chapel and then I will discharge him into your care.'

'But how did he survive? It's beyond belief he isn't dead!'

Comfrey hesitated. 'Having Luther around seemed to keep Penrose quiet.'

'Penrose!' The lawman almost spat in disgust. But, seeing that the warden's sparsely furnished office lacked a spittoon, he restrained himself. 'You put the boy in with that critter?'

Ambrose Penrose's wife had been murdered. Penrose, quite naturally, had dealt with the man suspected of doing the deed. Unfortunately evidence had been lacking and Penrose's method of dispatching the varmint had been enough to turn any decent man's stomach.

Penrose had been tried for murder, found guilty, and dispatched to the state penitentiary.

Comfrey shook his head. 'By rights the man would have been committed. But the asylum was damn reluctant to accept him.' He straightened his shoulders before announcing proudly, 'But I did my duty and housed him.'

'You said it yourself. The man belongs in an asylum. . . .' Standish's voice trailed away.

'I am sure my so doing kept Luther alive,' Comfrey, not liking criticism, replied sharply.

'Why's that?' Lawyer Robins questioned.

'Obviously with Larkin dead someone else would have been obliged to bunk with Penrose. And as no one wanted to be Penrose's cell-mate Luther's good health was assured. Why, I believe Penrose saw Luther as the son he might have had!'

'Well, let's get him out of here!' The lawman remembered the hot-headed youngster he'd initially been responsible for sending to this hell-hole.

Rising to his feet Comfrey summoned a guard and gave the necessary instructions.

'He'll be a free man. You can't force him back to Black Bear Crossing,' Robins snapped, mindful of the fact that Rancher Cooper had offered a commission to persuade Larkin to sell up and steer clear of his home town.

'Well, it seems we must wait while Luther says his prayers,' the Reverend Dent observed uncomfortably, well aware that he'd preached that the boy deserved to be hanged outright.

'The man sounds as though he has become a simpleton

whilst under your care, Warden Comfrey,' Robins accused, ill-pleased at being kept waiting.

Comfrey did not answer but pretended to busy himself with paperwork, leaving the three men to sit in uncomfortable silence.

It suddenly, and unwelcome, sprang into Standish's mind that maybe Larkin's duties involved cleaning out the prison latrines. Hadn't two men been murdered while using the latrine?

He kept silent. He'd railroaded young Luther Larkin, an innocent boy. He'd been so sure back then that Larkin had been guilty. He wasn't going to share his suspicions with Comfrey.

'So he gave up protesting his innocence?' Robins asked curiously.

'Luther always maintained that as he'd been found guilty he must be guilty even though he could not remember killing the Cooper boy,' Comfrey replied. 'He's always accepted his punishment. Now he's accepted that Walter Grainger was guilty all along and that that guilt made Grainger make his death bed confession, as witnessed by you three men.'

Standish remembered that a saloon woman whom Walt had been dallying with had arrived at the jailhouse insisting that the three men make their way out to Walt's ranch as a matter of urgency. Walt's time was coming, she'd said.

The door opened and a burly guard followed by a tall, thin young man entered Comfrey's office.

'Well here he is, Warden,' the guard said unnecessarily.

Comfrey waved a hand. 'You're not needed.' The guard withdrew.

13

*

Luther Larkin regarded the three men responsible for his sojourn in the penitentiary, the sheriff who had railroaded him, the lawyer who hadn't troubled to defend him and the preacher who had denounced him from the pulpit. As yet he was unsure what to do about these three. Penrose had suggested it was fitting that all three met an untimely end, to which Luther had replied that he aimed to play the cards as they were dealt.

He'd played those cards when he had first set eyes on Penrose. 'You keep me alive and I can get us both out of here,' he had said.

'I'm listening,' Penrose had responded and so an alliance had been formed.

'Well, Luther, here we are.' Comfrey smiled. 'Truth has prevailed and you're walking out of here a free man.'

'The Lord be praised,' Luther replied.

'Amen,' Comfrey replied piously.

Luther bowed his head, knowing that the Lord had nothing to do with any of this. Walt Grainger had confessed to something that Luther, upon reflection, still did not believe Walt had done. But sure as hell something had been troubling Walt to make him make that death-bed confession.

'Sit down.' Standish indicated a vacant chair.

Aware of their scrutiny, Luther sat waiting for one of them to express regret for the wrong that had been done to him all those years ago. No one did.

'Well. I believe we've thanked the Lord enough for today.' Robins sounded impatient.

I'm relying upon you to make Larkin see sense, Rancher Cooper had said. *There's nothing for him in Black Bear Crossing.*

This was not exactly true, as Luther had Walt's ranch. And now Cooper wanted that ranch, the land being a link between two stretches of land owned by Cooper. And of course there was the watering hole which locals called the Big Muddy.

Luther kept his eyes on his boots. He fought down the desire to lash out. Rage simmered inside like a volcano ready to erupt.

Maybe the lawman suspected how he was feeling. The man was no fool. Also, the fact that he was still around indicated a good deal of dexterity when it came to hauling iron.

'You're gonna have to learn to haul iron,' Penrose had declared. 'You're to find Clarence and take him along with you, because I cannot tote him along with me. The old varmint would slow me down plenty. But he'll be of use to you.'

'Well I—'

'You find Clarence. Do you hear me? I owe that old coot and I don't want to see him dead in an alleyway. You can be his purpose in life. And I'm telling you now, he ain't easy to get along with.'

Luther had nodded. He was stuck with Clarence. That was the way Penrose wanted it to be.

'So you see,' Lawyer Robins concluded, 'Marcus Cooper has authorized me to make you a generous offer for the ranch owned by the late Walter Grainger as an act of contrition willed to your good self.'

'Did you understand all that, Luther?' the Reverend Dent enquired kindly.

Luther raised his head. 'Yep,' he responded flatly.

'And I'd advise you not to accept.' Standish stuck in his oar. 'You'll come to grief. You've been shut up in this place too long. You need to learn to stand on your own two feet. I feel obliged to see you safely back to Black Bear Crossing.'

At last a hint of guilt, Luther thought.

'And you're absolutely right, Sheriff. We can head back to Black Bear Crossing this very day. But first there are things that I need to attend to.'

'You'll be looking for a woman, no doubt!' Robins smirked.

Luther shook his head. He could see they did not believe him. No matter. No need to explain that he must find an old drunk answering to the name of Clarence.

'About Rancher Cooper's offer. . . .' Robins tried again.

'I'll consider it once I'm back in Black Bear Crossing.'

'Well, I'll keep you company whilst you attend to your concerns,' Standish declared in a voice that did not brook argument.

'Fine by me,' Luther agreed. He knew the lawman would not let him out of his sight until they got back to Black Bear Crossing; his conscience, it seemed, was troubling him plenty.

Standish nodded. 'Best we head back as soon as we can then,' he observed, as yet unaware of the hours they would pass scouring every drinking establishment and nearby alleyway they could find.

*

'So how do you know this old coot?' Standish asked. Larkin had led him into numerous drinking establishments and stinking alleyways before they had at last discovered the near-insensible old bum.

At Larkin's insistence a horse and buggy had been bought. Luther Larkin had loaded the old drunk into the buggy where he had promptly passed out. And now he lay insensible, thanks be, beneath a blanket and stinking like a skunk.

If Standish had had anything to do with it they would have left old Clarence where they had found him, passed out amongst the garbage belonging to an establishment called the Red Lady Drinking Parlour.

'I don't!' Luther didn't bother to lie.

'But you're hell bent on toting him back to Black Bear Crossing.'

'Well, I guess Penrose feels responsible for the old varmint,' Luther responded.

'What the hell has Penrose got to do with you now, Luther?' the lawman demanded, jaw dropping open with surprise.

'Only a fool crosses Penrose.' Luther shrugged. 'That's how it is, lawman. If Penrose says I must take Clarence back to Black Bear Crossing that's what I'm gonna do!'

'Goddamn Penrose,' the old coot suddenly bellowed belligerently from the back of the buggy.

'He said you'd thank him when you sober up,' Luther pacified. 'And now I reckon it's time to head on back to Black Bear Crossing.' He turned away from his travelling companions. Right now he felt like spitting into their eyes, for these three men had so self-righteously consigned him to a living hell. 'Let's ride!'

Lord knows this day has been long in coming, he thought. He was not thinking of his vindication. For years whenever he had the chance he'd taken impressions of the keys. As a simpleton who'd walked around praying to himself guards had scarce spared him a glance. It had been a long and dangerous business. Now Penrose had the last of the keys. Tonight the penitentiary would go up in flames. Men would go free. 'I need necessary diversions,' Penrose had declared. Maybe innocent men would die. The men breaking out would be the worst kind of scum. They'd be hunted down eventually. But Luther knew that Ambrose Penrose would not be among them.

Daylight was fading as they made camp.

'I'll see to the horses.' Standish volunteered, wondering yet again why the old bum was with them.

Luther rested his back against the buggy wheel. He made no attempt to help with the preparation of stew and coffee. He simply watched the horizon.

'Look at that!' Robins pointed. A red glow had become visible against the grey of the sky.

Robins and Dent were not quick to work out what was going on but the sheriff knew instantly.

'The damn penitentiary is going up in flames. Goddamn!' he yelled. 'The scum have set the place ablaze. They're making a break for it.' He swung round to face Luther. 'What the hell do you know about this?'

'I know as much as you, which is nothing!'

'You heard him, you polecat,' the old man had clambered down from the buggy. Through bleary eyes he

18

regarded them.

'You varmint.' Standish seized the old coot by the shirt. He wouldn't have hurt the man, he just wanted to shut him up.

'Big mistake, lawman.' Cold steel pressed against Standish's belly. The oldster had drawn a knife. 'Now get your hands off my goddamn shirt.'

Carefully the lawman released the old man. He saw that Larkin had sprung to his feet. It was pretty clear that if violence erupted Larkin would be siding with the oldster.

'So that's the way of it?'

'I reckon,' Luther agreed.

Standish regarded the oldster thoughtfully. 'I guess,' he observed, 'that way back before you turned into a drunken old bum you were a mighty accomplished killer.'

The oldster shrugged. 'I was never a man to brag,' he rejoined. 'But folk walked wary around me. Now get me a mug of coffee.'

'Get it yourself,' Luther told him. 'You stink like a polecat, and that's coming from a man who has spent his best years incarcerated.'

Clarence cackled, amused by the response.

'We must hope the escapees will be hunted down and slaughtered like the mad dogs they are,' Robins looked around nervously. 'We'll set watch, of course.'

'The majority of men, if one can call them men, making a break for freedom will indeed be hunted down,' Standish observed. 'But this ain't about the majority of men. They are just a diversion. This is all about Ambrose Penrose. But you know that, don't you, Luther?'

Luther shrugged. 'Like I've said, I know no more than

you about what's going on back at the penitentiary.'

'I'd say keys have been cut,' the lawman essayed.

Luther shrugged.

'And I'd say you know something about that,' the lawman pressed on.

Standish was damn right. It had taken many long years getting the impressions of the keys needed to get out of the hell-hole. Penrose had seen to the cutting of the keys; once smuggled back inside those keys had been squirrelled away until the time was right.

The prison chapel had made a mighty useful hiding-place, hence Luther's religious zeal.

Indeed, if Walt Grainger had not made that deathbed confession Luther himself would be one of the mad dogs making a break for freedom.

CHAPTER 2

Luther was doing his damnest to ignore Clarence. They were seated on the porch of Walt Grainger's run-down ranch house.

'What's the matter with you, boy?' Clarence shook his head. 'Ain't it about time you avenged yourself on those three polecats. If I was in your boots, I'd have their guts. If a man does you a wrong he must pay for it.'

'Well, I ain't as vengeful as you, Clarence. At heart I am not a killer.'

Clarence poured another mug of black coffee. 'Hell, it is hard being sober,' he observed. 'Every time I look in the mirror I see an old coot, not the hell-raiser I once was.' He took a mouthful of coffee. 'You say you are not a killer, but I can tell you with certainty you will have to kill to survive. This town ain't friendly disposed towards you, I'd say. You remind them of the wrong they done you. And of course, there's the ranch. I'd guess Marcus Cooper is looking to expand and you are in his way. He'll want to be rid of you and that's a fact.'

'I can't help that.'

21

'And as for Standish, he has cottoned on to the fact thst the jailbreak could not have happened without your endeavours. He'll turn against you, if he ain't already.'

'Who the hell cares?' Luther rejoined. He took a deep breath. 'I'm forgoing vengeance. I want no part of it. I've seen enough violence inside the state penitentiary to last a lifetime.' He shook his head. 'Innocent folk are dying on account of me.'

'What innocent folk?'

'Some of the cons will be on a killing spree. That's for sure.'

Clarence shrugged. 'But they'll be hunted down and lynched. Good folk will have themselves a killing spree. Maybe stand the corpses in their open coffins on the sidewalk and have themselves photographed with the dead.' He shook his head. 'But Ambrose will get clean away. You knew this was how things had to be. You did what had to be done and that's all there is to it. And don't forget, if Standish had done his job, if the goddamn two-bit town had not railroaded you, why, you would not have been in the penitentiary in the first place.'

The oldster stared into the distance.

'You did a mighty fine job. Just remind yourself it was either that or spend the rest of your life rotting away for a killing you did not commit. You weren't to know this Walt Grainger would up and make a deathbed confession. And what else could you do but honour your pledge to Ambrose Penrose? Without him around you would never have lasted in that hell-hole.'

'That's true enough.'

'Now put it out of your mind.'

Luther nodded, his expression grim.

'You want to live a peaceable life you say. And you aim to keep this ranch?'

'I sure do.'

'Well, the way I see it, that's dependent upon other folks allowing you to lead a peaceable life. This here Marcus Cooper wants your ranch. Hell, he might even have been the one to kill his own brother, for avarice makes many cross the line. Why, Walt Grainger might have had his suspicions. Whatever the truth of it, the man had a powerful reason for clearing your name and Cooper will not be best pleased. So now you must ask yourself the question: do you think Cooper will let you be? *He* sure as hell won't. He wants Walt's spread real bad. Why else would he have sent the lawyer fellow along to make you an offer?'

'You're sounding mighty cheerful,' Luther observed. Realization dawned. 'You're hoping for trouble, ain't you?'

'I sure am. And that's why Ambrose Penrose had me tag along. He knew I'd welcome becoming involved in a fracas. When you make old bones life ain't got much of a purpose and that's a fact.'

'I'm surprised you made old bones.'

'Well, the late Mrs Duffy, my lady wife, ordered me to stop my killing ways and I did whilst she was around.' His eyes misted at past recollections. 'I was given to violent rage, you see, and she would have none of it.' He eyed Luther curiously. 'I ain't seen you real mad yet.'

'And you won't, neither, for I am not given to foolish rage.'

'This is a violent land. It ain't a place for the weak.' With that Clarence jumping to his feet and lashed out with his walking cane.

The blow caught Luther across the legs. Biting back a howl he lurched to his feet.

'You're loco, Clarence. You're a crazy old coot!'

Clarence lashed out again and Luther dodged the blow.

'You damn varmint, Clarence!'

'Now if you were wearing a Peacemaker I'd not be lashing out,' Clarence yelled. 'I've no time for a man who shows scant interest in learning to handle a Peacemaker. And keeps his temper.'

'We're gonna talk this through, Clarence. Ain't I explained I've seen enough violence to last me through until I end my day?'

'Well, you won't have many days left to you. I can't believe you have turned into a holy Joe, a galoot who goes around yapping about forgiveness, a man who ignores the danger coming his way.'

Abruptly the oldster halted his deranged assault.

'What danger?'

'Just turn your head you, damn idiot, for we have riders headed our way. You've got visitors.'

Luther turned his head. It was a mistake. The stick cracked across his legs and brought him to his knees. He lay in the dirt, his legs throbbing with pain. But the old coot had not been lying. Riders were indeed heading their way. Even after all this time he recognized the big man in the lead. It was Marcus Cooper.

Marcus Cooper had grown into a large, powerfully built *hombre*. The four men riding with him looked to be hardcases. Feeling a damn fool Luther scrambled to his feet, ashamed they'd witnessed him being bested by a crazy old coot. Clarence, he saw, was heading back towards the house. But the oldster wasn't running from trouble, as Cooper might be imagining if indeed he was paying the oldster any heed.

Walt Grainger had owned a buffalo gun! Clarence had given his attention to the weapon, saying how it wasn't only four-legged critters it was good for.

Bunched tightly together the group came to a halt. Intimidating scowls were directed Luther's way as the men regarded him with ill-concealed contempt.

Hell, he was a goddamn fool. He'd been caught out in the open, unarmed. Helpless! Suddenly he was glad the crazy old man was around. The old coot would not hesitate to blast away with the buffalo gun. Nor would Clarence worry about hitting Luther.

'That's your bad luck,' the oldster would say. Killing, after all, had been Clarence's forte. It would not bother him none.

The sun had tanned Cooper's skin, whereas Luther remained pallid and unhealthy-looking. He felt strangely detached; this confrontation, for confrontation it was, could only end in one of two ways. Marcus Cooper would take his men and ride away. If not, the only man left alive was going to be the oldster.

Nor did Luther care if he and Marcus Cooper were destined to meet their maker on this very pleasant sunny day.

But Marcus Cooper would care about dying. That was, Luther saw, an important difference between them. Cooper's men would likewise care.

Clarence wouldn't give a damn about any of them. The odds were not stacked in Cooper's favour. Soon the rancher would find this out.

'Well, who would have thought it,' Cooper declared when Luther did not speak. 'Who would have thought that it was Walt Grainger after all who killed my kid brother?'

'You tell me,' Luther rejoined calmly. 'You're a man, after all, who has all the answers.'

'I'm giving you a choice, Larkin. Saddle up and ride out of here and I'll let you live. I'm damned put out, I can tell you, that you saw fit to decline my offer to buy you out. We don't want your kind in Black Bear Crossing. There are some of us who believe Walt Grainger was not in his right mind when he made his deathbed confession.' Marcus Cooper was evidently not a man to waste time on pleasantries.

'You damn fool of a varmint, Luther Larkin,' a voice bellowed from the ranch house.

'Don't mind Clarence. You interrupted his fun,' Luther said. 'Yep, he sure is in an evil frame of mind right now.'

'Now there's nothing to stop me blasting you,' the rancher continued as though they had not been interrupted, 'except I know you will choose right and ride out. I see you're not much of a man. Hell, your hired man—'

'Is a crazed old coot who is just longing for an opportunity to do what he does best!'

'What the hell are you talking about?'

'Some men like to kill. They do it for enjoyment. Maybe you're one such man or maybe not. But Clarence sure as hell is. Why the hell do you think he legged it for the house when he saw you men riding in? Right now that old

26

varmint don't give a damn about saving my hide or even his own. He's got us all covered with Walt's old buffalo gun. He's itching for you to make a move so that he can return the compliment. Fact is, if I holler out for him to start blasting away he will happily oblige.'

'You'd be caught in the line of fire,' a hardcase with Cooper observed. His small piglike eyes gleamed with. malice.

'Well, Clarence don't give a damn about me being in his line of fire. It ain't nothing personal. It's just that he's got a craving to use the buffalo gun. Men can get a hunger for killing, which never goes away no matter how many years pass.'

'Are you saying your hired man would gun you down?' Cooper evidenced disbelief.

'Well, he ain't exactly my hired man. But yes, he'd gun me down without batting an eye. He ain't my pard and I ain't his pard. We're both destined for hell and neither one of us gives a damn. Can you say the same, Marcus Cooper, you and your men?'

'You're a damn cowardly skunk, Luther Larkin!' Pig-eyes accused. 'What kind of yellow belly lets a crazy old coot set about him with a stick.'

Luther ignored the damn fool question. He continued to regard Marcus Cooper.

'Well, that's it to be? It's your call. Are you gonna ride out and leave me be, or do you aim to join me in hell this very day.'

'I'm through waiting,' the oldster bellowed. 'I'm counting to twelve, then I aim to have myself a party.'

'He'll do it.' Luther spoke more to himself than to

Marcus Cooper. 'He ain't afraid of the consequences,'

'I've seen that old coot,' one of the hardcases observed. 'Years back it was. Hell, he don't give a damn who he blasts. Even womenfolk and kids counted for nothing where Clarence Duffy was concerned.'

Luther saw that Cooper was finally taking notice. Realization had dawned. He'd accepted that the oldster really would blast away and to hell with the consequences.

'I'm riding out. I've my crew to consider.' Cooper spat, the gob landed on Luther's shirt. 'Mighty soon the folk in Black Bear Crossing are gonna know you for the yellow-belly you are. That's a promise!' Yanking his horse around, Cooper viciously raked the animal with his silver star spurs before forking it out.

Whooping, the crew followed their boss.

Luther stared after them. A gauntlet had been thrown down. This wasn't over. There'd be more trouble to come.

'It's as clear as day that man won't let things be,' Clarence said as he joined him outside. 'I'd recommend that it is best to kill him sooner rather than later. Hell, if you were proficient with the Peacemaker you could call him out.' The old man shook his head. 'Too bad you ain't up to the job. Through no fault of your own. What do you say? Shall we find out if you have a talent for hauling iron?'

Luther nodded reluctantly. He saw no other way out of this mess. Pretty damn soon he'd be obliged to kill. Cooper would give him no other choice.

'Well Bert, can you do the job?' Marcus Cooper pushed a box of fine cigars towards the man sitting on the far side of his pride and joy, the big mahogany desk. 'Help your-self,' he offered with rare generosity.

'That's mighty generous of you, boss.' Bert Barlow took a handful of cigars. 'And as for being up to the job, I guess you're joshing. I'm your man.'

'Well, it shouldn't be that difficult for a man such as yourself. We've all seen that he is a yellow-belly. Whatever fighting spirit Larkin possessed was clearly knocked out of him during his incarceration.'

'True enough. The varmint lacks backbone,' Bert rejoined. 'I heard tell that whilst he was in the penitentiary he passed his time cleaning the latrines. Maybe that's why he survived.' Barlow guffawed. 'No one else wanted that goddamn job!'

Seeing that it was expected Cooper joined in the laughter.

'Now Bert, my problem is that Sheriff Standish is weighed down with guilt. For now he believes he's obliged to look out for Larkin. If you were to kill Larkin I'd have a problem with Standish. What I want you to do is make Larkin's guts twist with fear. I want the town to know him for the yellow-bellied coward he is. I want him shamed. I want him to leave town of his own accord.'

'You're letting him move on?'

'Hell no! We'll gun him down as he's headed out. We'll get him when he thinks he is safe. No one will know. No one will care.'

'I'd rather string him up. More fun that way,' Barlow rejoined.

'I don't give a damn how we get rid of hm.'

Barlow guffawed again. 'Now if you had asked me to

tangle with the oldster I would have been damned scared,' he joshed. 'But Larkin ain't worth a spit.'

'Good man. I knew I could count on you. Now get yourself to town. Check into the hotel and wait for the yellow-belly to show up.'

'Suppose he shows up with the old man?'

'Then you wait for another opportunity. Sooner or later he'll ride in solo. Hell, he can't hide out at the ranch indefinitely. He'll know he'll have to face the town. I'm a good judge of character. Standish is turning against Larkin. He blames him for the atrocities being committed by those damned escaped convicts. Our lawman won't be in any hurry to come to Luther's aid.'

'As soon as you set foot in town trouble will seek you out,' Clarence advised. 'And I ain't sure you can handle it.'

'You may be right.'

'I know I'm right.'

'You're looking pretty damn cheerful, Clarence.'

'Well, I sure am, Luther. The old days were the best years of my life. I've gunned down more than I can remember. I feel that leastways for the time being the old days are back.' He seemed to consider. 'Now I'd advise you not to wear a Peacemaker. You're getting there but you ain't there yet. So, I'm gonna give you my old skinning knife. I'd say you're more comfortable with a blade.'

'Well, I reckon I am. It was always a weapon of preference at the penitentiary.'

'You'll have surprise on your side, for you don't look much of any kind of threat.'

'You ain't riding in with me?'

'No. It's important you do this alone. It's important that this two-bit town recognize you ain't a man to be messed with. Hell, you don't want every no-account bum thinking they can insult you with impunity. It's time for you to walk tall! You ain't that boy that had his head pushed into a slop bucket.'

Luther took the knife. He stared at the blade's serrated and stained edge. He could easily imagine the oldster plunging this blade into flesh and then twisting viciously, seeking to tear organs beyond repair.

'I ain't,' he agreed.

'Now, you don't pull this blade unless it's gonna be used to kill. It ain't for show or putting a scare into folk. And lest you forget I'm gonna remind you of the number one rule when it comes to staying alive. Which is?' he prompted.

'Finish them first time.' Reluctantly he took the blade. His stomach churned as he remembered Silas Wright, the snitch. Wright had gotten wind that an attempted break-out was imminent. But he hadn't suspected that the jail simpleton was a pivotal part of that plot. He'd never suspected that Luther was going to be the one to end his life.

'Get the hell out,' he had said when Luther entered the latrines. Those had been his very last words.

'We don't leave our enemies around to fight another day,' Clarence broke in on Luther's thoughts. 'We don't give them another chance to finish us off. Now if you want to humiliate yourself by eating humble pie to avoid confrontation, well, I can see that might be your way of trying to avoid trouble. Maybe it will work. Maybe it won't. It would not be my way but I can see you ain't like me.'

'I ain't eating humble pie. It don't work!'

'And ask yourself, do you think anyone in that two-bit town gives a damn about you? Oh sure, some might be feeling guilty for putting an innocent boy away. But the guilt will not last long and soon they will be convincing themselves that it was your own damn fault. They'll be saying there was something not quite right about you and they cannot be blamed for making wrong assumptions.'

'You're crazy, Clarence.'

'I am what life has made me. I was an orphan boy, Luther. Taken in and used as a damn slave by a dirt farmer who wanted a hired man working for free. The whole town knew he was beating me black and blue. No one said a word.' The old man shook his head. 'Hell, that farmer and his wife screamed like pigs and then, when I'd finished, I fed their remains to the hogs. I ain't never looked back. I've played the cards as they were dealt and so must you. Now get yourself into town and buy our supplies. It's time to show folk you can stand on your own two feet. You are your own man now. There's nothing to stop you heading for the saloon and seeking the acquaintance of those sporting women.'

Luther held his peace. There was only one woman he was interested in and she would not be found in any saloon.

As he rode into town he saw folk eyeing him curiously. Instinct told him some of them knew something that he did not. He was not scared; after state penitentiary two-bit townfolk counted for nothing. Last time he'd been in this town it had seemed that every inhabitant had been baying for his blood.

'Luther!' a voice called as he was about to enter the general store. The Reverend Dent was headed his way. 'It's good to see you.' Dent shook him by the hand. 'I hope to see you at divine service,' Dent continued.

'Well, maybe,' Luther replied cautiously.

'But not that old man! He's beyond redemption.' Dent spoke pompously.

'Wild horses wouldn't get Clarence inside your church.' Luther smiled. 'But I am warning you now, don't ever take it into your head to denounce Clarence from your pulpit like you did me. I ain't forgotten. But then I am a forgiving man. Clarence ain't.'

'What are you saying,' the minister blustered.

'I know you like to single out folk for mention. But there's some folk best left be if you want to keep a tongue in your head.' Luther winked. 'And Clarence is crazy enough to cut that tongue right out of your mouth.'

Ignoring Dent's shocked expression he entered the store.

Silence fell inside the place. He knew he was the centre of attention.

'We don't all believe Walt Grainger's confession,' a bonnet-wearing farmer's wife observed, glaring at him boldly as if daring him to react.

Kenna, the grizzled storekeeper glared at Luther from behind the counter. Slightly behind her husband Mrs Kenna stood to attention, gimlet eyes fixed on Luther.

'No credit!' Kenna pointed to the sign.

Luther placed the list on the counter. 'I see you ain't changed. Just get my supplies and quit gabbing. I've got money to pay.'

'I'm glad to hear that, Luther. You know it's nothing personal.' Kenna scrutinized the list, then, removing a stub of pencil from behind his ear, he rapidly jotted down the cost.

Luther paid up without being asked. He waited while the goods were taken down from the shelves. Then, feeling the devil inside him taking the opportunity, he stepped back and trod heavily on the foot of the farmer's wife, for she was crowding his space, watching his every move.

'Beg pardon, ma'am,' he apologized as she cried out in pain. She at least had gotten her just deserts.

'All ready, Luther. I will help you load the buggy,' Kenna offered.

Mrs Kenna sidled close. 'Amos Standish has been called out of town,' she hissed. 'He left with one of Rancher Cooper's men. If you've any sense you'll get out of here as fast as you can.' She hesitated. 'I always thought you were innocent.'

'Why didn't you say so?'

'Well, Kenna believes we should mind our own business.'

Before he could respond Luther became aware that there was a commotion outside the store. 'I guess a whole parcel of folk aim to mind their own business,' he observed wearily. 'Unless I am mistaken trouble is headed my way.'

Stepping outside he saw that a crowd was gathering on Main Street. Some of the galoots wore unpleasant expressions that spoke more than words. Beneath their bonnets some of the women looked plain excited. He knew he was going to provide the entertainment.

Advancing along Main Street was a huge giant of a man. A man Luther had seen earlier; Cooper's man, and that could only mean all hell was about to break out.

'Damnation,' Luther muttered under his breath. He'd be obliged to use the knife. Fists would not suffice against this giant.

He wished the ground would open up and swallow him whole. No way did he want to draw that lethal blade. But he recognized that it had to be done.

CHAPTER 3

'You're gonna wish you stayed away.'

Luther recognized the voice. It belonged to Higgy Shaw, town troublemaker.

'That's Bert Barlow. He works for Mr Cooper.'

'I know that, Higgy.'

'Let me tell you there are some of us folk who believe Walt was out of his mind when he confessed to killing Hamish Cooper.'

Luther's eyes narrowed speculatively. 'You told lies about me, Higgy. I ain't forgotten. Take care you don't get your just deserts!'

'No. I never did.' Higgy, true to form, denied the accusation.

'One day you and me are gonna have a talk. But not right now. I've got more important matters than you on my mind.'

'How did you like the penitentiary?' Higgy jeered, backing away. 'Your threats don't scare me!'

'I ain't threatening you, Higgy.' Luther paused. 'Because you ain't worth a spit and we both know it.'

Bert Barlow's intentions were plain. He was looking for trouble.

'You're a damned yellow-belly,' Bert bellowed. 'You're too damn yellow even to strap on a Peacemaker. Hell, Luther Larkin, you ain't any kind of man.' With a flourish Bert deliberately unbuckled his gunbelt. 'I'm too much of a man to gun down an unarmed varmint. Ain't that right?' he appealed to the engrossed spectators.

This was following a predictable pattern, Luther thought as he listened to the murmurs of agreement from the watching men.

'Now there's plenty in town who believe Walt had gone mad with pain when he made his deathbed confession. I say we don't want your kind in our town. I say it would be in your best interests to ride out. You can't hide behind Sheriff Standish for ever. I say you're still a guilty man, Luther Larkin. I say every decent citizen in this town wants you gone.'

A woman screamed as Barlow pulled out his blade. Voices yelled out words of encouragement, but not for Luther.

'We're with you, Bert,' Higgy Shaw yelled.

'Are you here to kill me then, Bert?' Luther enquired. He felt strangely calm. He did not believe Barlow was under orders to kill him. A hunch told him that Marcus Cooper would not want to look bad.

The rancher would be wary of openly tangling with the lawman. And as the sheriff was not in Cooper's pocket it seemed likely that Standish had been deliberately lured away from town on a wild-goose chase.

Across Main Street Reverend Dent and Lawyer Robins

watched the proceedings. Neither was man enough to intervene. Their shocked expressions told Luther that they were not coming to his aid.

'There ain't no need for you to wet your pants, Larkin. All I want is a word.' Barlow advanced, a smirk upon his face. He was confident; too damn confident for his own good. Right now the man was thinking that Luther Larkin was not worth a spit.

Resting his back against the rough wall of the telegraph office, Luther waited. From the corner of his eye he spotted Higgy Shaw sidling closer, no doubt wanting a ringside seat for the free show. Luther was also shocked to see that so-called respectable females were in the crowd, jostling the men for a good view of the proceedings.

'Please . . .' Luther croaked, deciding he did not want a protracted knife fight on Main Street. For one thing, were Bert seen to be losing Bert's pards were capable of stepping in to tip the scales. It was best to get this fracas over pretty damn quick. With the element of surprise on his side he'd pull through.

'Please,' Bert mimicked scornfully.

'Don't kill me. . . .' Luther knew he sounded pathetic. That particular ploy had worked well in the state penitentiary until folks wised up.

'You ain't worth a spit.' Clearly a showman, Bert switched his mean-looking blade hand to hand. 'Admit you ain't worth a spit. And then you sign the papers drawn up by Robins. Collect your money from the bank and ride out. We don't want your kind in our town. No sir, that we don't!'

'I ain't worth a spit,' Luther mumbled.

Guffawing with laughter Bert moved that important step closer and spat into Luther's face.

'That's learning him,' Higgy yelled gleefully without realizing what was about to happen.

Making his move Luther came to life. He lunged forward. His left hand had already pulled the concealed blade whilst his right wiped the gob of foul spit that had hit him squarely in the eye. He didn't need to see particularly well to plunge the blade with all the force he could muster into Bert's overhanging belly. A vicious blow to Bert's face sent the huge man reeling backwards. He hit the ground with a thud, his shirt darkening with blood.

Luther stepped forward and jerked his blade free of Bert's flesh, giving a vicious twist as he pulled the steel clear.

One of Bert's pards was reaching for his gun. Without even having to think about it Luther hurled the blade with deadly accuracy, catching the waddy mid-throat. Blood spurted, splashing those close to the doomed man. A woman screamed as the dead man fell face downwards into the dirt.

'Who else,' Luther yelled, snatching up Bert's discarded gunbelt and quickly buckling it around his waist.

No one moved. They gawked at him, mouths dropping open with astonishment. None of them had been expecting this particular outcome. If anyone had asked he could have told them that the blade had always been the weapon of the penitentiary. Doubtless there were many on Main Street who could outshoot him, but they didn't know it and he wasn't about to tell them.

Bert was done for. He'd quickly bled out and now

Rancher Cooper's tool was no more use. When the rancher heard of his man's demise he would curse the fellow for being an incompetent fool, because that was the kind of man Cooper was.

With a curse Luther pulled the blade from the downed waddy's throat. He wiped it clean on the man's waistcoat before returning it to the sheath. Then his gaze fell on an ashen-faced Higgy Shaw.

'See that pile of horse droppings. Well, Higgy, I want you to mosey over and stick your face in that pile. When you've done that you can get out of my sight. You're getting off lightly and you know it. Your damn lies helped get me railroaded. Go on now, before I change my mind and blast you where you stand.'

As he had expected no one stepped forward to tell him to leave Higgy be. He watched as Higgy, always the coward, obeyed the command. Then, face coated with muck, Higgy dashed for a nearby alleyway. Hoots and jeers from the spectators followed his departure.

Across Main Street, Dent and Robins continued to gawk with disbelief.

'Well, they all know the kind of man they are dealing with,' Kenna observed gruffly as he quickly loaded the last of Luther's order. 'And I guess our lawman does too, for here he is, just as the dust is settling.'

Riding down Main Street, Sheriff Standish was quick to realize that he'd been duped by Marcus Cooper. The wide-loopers supposedly penned up in one of the canyons by the rancher's men had seemingly vanished into thin air. The lawman had wasted a hell of a lot of time finding this out.

Two dead men, blood pooling beneath them, lay on the dirt of Main Street. Standish knew then that the galoot who had returned to Black Bear Crossing in no way resembled young Luke Larkin. This man had killed and was not troubled by it.

Luther Larkin kept his lips buttoned as folk surged around the lawman, all wanting to voice their own version of events.

'So it seems Bert instigated the confrontation,' Amos Standish drawled as he confronted Luther.

'Well, I guess the luckless fool was merely following orders,' Luther rejoined.

'And now he's dead,' the lawman concluded.

'His own damn fault, I'd say.'

'Well, I'd say that until now no one in town knew what kind of man you had turned into,' the lawman noted sourly. 'I can see that you are no stranger to violence.'

'Well, I'd say any thinking man ought to have known violence is endemic in the state penitentiary.'

'We can talk in my office. You vultures, get those two dead men toted to the undertaker.' Standish strode away without waiting to see if Luther would follow.

'Sure,' Luther agreed. He followed Standish into the law office. Last time he'd been in here the sheriff had been railroading him, refusing to believe that he'd only found a dead Hamish Cooper; that the blood on his hands was from trying to help. It hadn't helped that Luther's pa had been the town drunk and that Higgy Shaw had gone around town telling folk he'd heard Luther Larkin threatening to kill Hamish Cooper because young Maybelle Grainger was walking out with Hamish, having refused

41

Luther's invite to the town picnic.

'Say, Sheriff, what the hell became of my pa?' Luther asked before the sheriff could speak.

'Why, he passed on. We found him froze to death in an alleyway one winter's morning. They'd thrown him out of the saloon and he'd been unable to get home under his own steam.'

'Well, that figures.'

'I'm guessing you killed those *hombres* back in the state penitentiary. That was your doing!' Standish accused. 'They got wind that you and Penrose were planning to break out!'

'Hell, lawman, are you asking me to incriminate myself? Do you take me for a fool? You'll get no confession out of me.'

'I take you for a dangerous varmint!'

'A man does what needs to be done to stay alive. If you'd been incarcerated in the state penitentiary you would know what I am taking about,' Luther rejoined grimly. 'It's thanks to you and this two-bit town that I was incarcerated in the penitentiary.'

'You know Marcus Cooper won't let this be.' Standish was clearly disinclined to talk about the way he had rail-roaded Luther.

'Cooper must want Walt's old spread real bad. I guess he wants to get his hands on the Big Muddy. As I recall whoever controls that watering hole in times of drought holds the cards. I guess Cooper must want to see his neighbours go under. He's keen to expand his empire,' Luther surmised.

'Yep, he's got big ideas.' The lawman paused. 'It seems

you don't need protection from me!'

'I often took a dip in the Big Muddy when I was a youngster,' Luther reminisced, ignoring the remark. 'Walt Grainger's pa tried to shoot me one time for dipping in his water. He weren't joshing. I thought I was done for. I was scared real bad.' He smiled at the memory of a happier time. Then his smile faded. 'That's what I was doing at the water hole that day. It was a damn scorcher, I recall. I'd gone there to take a dip and there was Hamish Cooper with his skull caved in. I was so damn shaken I did not know what to do. Then, before I knew it, folk were accusing me. I can see now that was because my pa was the town drunk and we were damn poor.'

'Well, now we know it was Walt Grainger all along.' Standish spoke defensively, clearly unwilling to chew over the past.

'Say, Sheriff, what happened to Walt's sister?'

'The girl you were sweet on!'

Luther shrugged.

'Well, you had best put her out of your mind. Maybelle married Marcus Cooper. Walt and Marcus were brothers-in-law.'

'Well, if that don't beat all! Was there bad feeling between Walt and Marcus?'

'Not as far as I know!'

Luther's thoughts drifted. He had asked Maybelle to the town picnic but she'd refused him, telling him a dirt-poor farmer's boy wasn't good enough to lick her boots. She'd gone with Hamish Cooper.

But Luther had not harboured ill feeling towards Hamish. The second son of a prosperous rancher, Hamish was clearly a better catch than the son of a town drunk.

'I know you killed Hamish,' Standish had accused. 'Higgy Shaw has come forward to say he heard you vowing to make Hamish Cooper pay for stealing your girl.'

'But Maybelle was not my girl,' Luther had argued. 'Sure, I asked her to the town picnic, but she turned me down. That was her right and I was man enough to accept her decision.'

'You are no man,' Standish had bellowed. 'And didn't you tell Maybelle Grainger she'd be sorry if she walked out with Hamish?'

'I never did.'

'You're a damn liar, boy. I know one when I see one. You're gonna confess. You hear me now?'

Then Standish had got out the slop bucket and Luther's ordeal had commenced. He'd never confessed but he'd sure as hell stopped protesting his innocence because that had inflamed Standish even further.

'Of course, with Hamish dead Marcus would inherit the whole damn ranch,' Luther spat. 'But you never even considered that possibility did you, Sheriff.'

'And I ain't considering it now,' Standish rejoined. 'It is pure nonsense to imply that Marcus killed his younger brother. Walt had a motive, after all. For all we know Walt did not cotton to Hamish sniffing around his sister. Let sleeping dogs be, Luther.'

'Well, you ain't changed. You're still not interested in the truth. Keep out of my path, lawman. I ain't forgotten what you did all those years back.'

'Are you threatening me?'

'Nope! And I never threatened Hamish Cooper.'

'I suggest you get on home. I'll have words with Cooper. I'll let him know that when it comes to the law he is not above the law. I'm an honest lawman, Luther Larkin. I believed you to be guilty!'

'You took the easy way out. Hamish's pa was leaning on you. I was the easiest option.'

'Think what you like. Now get out of my office.'

Driving back to the ranch Luther recognized that he could not avoid the trouble headed his way. He'd strapped on a Peacemaker and there was no going back. He had to be ready and able to use the weapon. Marcus Cooper would not let matters lie.

His cellmate Ambrose Penrose had rightly anticipated that trouble would come knocking at the door. That was why he'd insisted that Luther tote Clarence along, not to save the oldster from rot-gut booze, as Luther had supposed, but to prepare Luther for the fight ahead.

He found himself thinking about Maybelle, although he knew he was a fool for doing so. As decent folk attended Sunday service, doubtless Mrs Cooper, as she was now, would be coming to town for the service. With this in mind wild horses would not keep him away from Dent's church.

Idly, he found himself wondering whether it would be possible to entice her away from Marcus Cooper. A man could always hope.

You damn fool Luther. Forget about that woman! He could almost hear the voice of his cellmate, convicted killer Ambrose Penrose.

And you were a fool, he remembered Penrose telling him.

You should have left Hamish Cooper where you found him instead of heading for town with your duds soaked in a dead man's blood! You sure as hell made a convenient scapegoat.

'I'm telling you now I aim to attend Sunday service. I ain't missing it.' Luther had waited until the last moment to inform the oldster of his intentions.

'Well, I understand you'd like to hold two fingers up to that two-bit town, but you have more important matters to attend to. You ain't up to gunfighter standard and that's a fact,' Clarence argued, clearly expecting Luther to acquiesce.

'I aim to take a look at Miz Maybelle. I want to see if she's as pretty as I remember.'

To Luther's surprise Clarence merely nodded.

'Go right ahead. But don't you be forgetting she's another man's wife. She ain't the girl you've remembered all these years. And don't you be forgetting you never even knew that girl. She never spoke up for you, did she? She never said you were innocent.'

'Luther, welcome!' Dent's words rang false. The minister was at the church door, welcoming members of his congregation as they arrived.

'What brings you here, Luther Larkin?' someone asked.

'I'm here for the same reason as the rest of you. To hear Reverend Dent preach,' he prevaricated.

'Say, Luther, weren't you scared in the state penitentiary?' a freckle-faced youngster piped up as his mother pulled him into the church. 'I wish I'd seen you kill Bert Barlow,' the youngster yelled.

Luther ignored the kid. He entered the church, deliberately ignoring the looks directed his way. But he knew damn well that even in a place of worship a man was not necessarily safe. So, much as he wanted to take a front side pew he took a back seat, prudently putting the wall at his back.

He watched the sheriff arrive with a soup-faced woman on his arm, presumably Mrs Standish. Likewise the lawyer Robins had a woman on his arm. Luther had not realized that both these men were now married. Hell, if he had not been railroaded he might well be sitting here with a wife of his own: although probably not Maybelle. She'd been aiming high, wanting to bag herself a ranching man, and that was just what she'd done.

Rage churned in his belly. He fought it down. Hell, he wanted to blast the three men he blamed for his wrongful conviction. He wanted to smash up this two-bit town, fire his shooter and see folk run for their lives. Crazy thought, he knew.

As for Warden Comfrey, who'd made his life hell until Luther had transformed himself into a religious zealot who wanted nothing more than to clean stinking latrines and stinking cells, well, Comfrey would be answering to Ambrose Penrose soon enough.

Yes sir, Comfrey had made a mistake in humiliating Ambrose Penrose every chance he got. Penrose had not cared to be exhibited like a caged animal. But Penrose would strike when it was least expected. Nor would he draw attention to himself.

Forcing himself to relax, Luther adopted what he hoped was a pleasant expression, and just in time, for at that very moment a vision of loveliness in dark-green velvet walked into the church.

Maybelle was here. Unfortunately she was on her husband's arm.

A ripple of expectancy ran through the church. Eyes were on Cooper, watching to see what he aimed to do about Luther Larkin. But Marcus Cooper looked neither to right nor left as he walked slowly towards his place of importance in the front row. But Maybelle, turning her head, smiled at Luther.

'Luther, I am so glad that the injustice done to you has been righted,' she said clearly for everyone to hear. 'Welcome to our church.' With that she continued on her way.

He could not help but feel tremendously pleased that she had spoken to him. She could have ignored him but she had not. Although maybe she'd only spoken to him to make her husband mad. Survival in the state penitentiary meant ulterior motives had always to be expected.

Folk got to their feet as Dent announced the hymn to be sung. Luther, amusing himself at the town's expense, joined in. He'd been told he had a fine singing voice.

He stifled a smile. Hell, he could always take to the trail as a roaming preacher, persuading folk to part with their cash, for no one knew the good book better than he. But he couldn't do it. That damn fool Marcus Cooper had made his move and Luther was damned if he would back away. No way, after the fracas with that damn idiot Bert Barlow, was Cooper getting hold of Walt's spread.

A dishevelled woman burst screaming into the church. She stumbled down the aisle and collapsed against the base of Dent's pulpit, causing the hymn singing to fade away to be replaced by stunned silence as folk noticed the muck plastered over her head and gown.

A man sniggered, then hurriedly turned the sound into a cough.

'Look what she's done to me,' the woman screamed. 'It was her! Timberlee! She was watching out for me. From the saloon balcony! She set a trap. I was hurrying. I knew I was a trifle late. I didn't see her, didn't know what she was about until she emptied the contents of her chamber pot over me.'

The freckle-faced kid sidled gleefully up to Luther. Evidently he'd got away from his ma.

'It's Mrs Fenton, our schoolmarm,' he began, but he said no more, for his mother who'd given pursuit soundly boxed his ears.

'That creature needs committing. Only a madwoman would do what she's done.' Luther was disappointed to see that the speaker was Maybelle.

Voices concurred. Women rushed to surround a now sobbing Mrs Fenton, to hide her from view. Maybelle, Luther noted, took the lead. For a moment amusement had flitted across Maybelle's face, to be replaced quickly by sympathy.

Dent's Sunday service was more than he had expected. He guessed that Mrs Fenton must have done something to incur this Miz Timberlee's ire, but no one was concerned about that.

Women went going crazy for nothing much at all, he thought. They all seemed to be on their feet crying out that something must be done. He watched bemused as they berated the men for their inactivity on this matter.

Sheriff Amos Standish, now on his feet, looked mighty uncomfortable.

'Well, this ain't exactly a job for the law,' he griped.

'That's where you are wrong, Amos Standish,' a woman screamed. Luther saw that it was Standish's wife doing the yelling. It occurred to him then that things could turn unpleasant. Mobs turned ugly soon enough and these 'good' folk gave every appearance of turning into an angry mob.

CHAPTER 4

Luther was the last to leave the church. He joined Kenna and the two of them watched the 'mob' storm down Main Street.

'So what's all this ruckus about?' Luther asked.

Kenna shook his head, 'It seems those two women met head on whilst on the sidewalk and neither would give way. And then the schoolmarm, encouraged by a no-account meddler, shoved Miz Timberlee off.'

'Well it seems she has had her revenge,' Luther observed, unable to suppress a grin.

'Problem is folk in this town ain't laughing.' Kenna shrugged. 'Miz Timberlee is in big trouble. So I'd get on out of town if I were you,' the storekeeper continued. 'It would be the best thing you could do.'

Luther looked to where the storekeeper was gazing. With a jolt he realized what Kenna was telling him. Miz Timberlee had hidden beneath the tarp covering his supplies. She was in his buggy, and there was nothing he could do about it. He could not denounce the woman and see her at the mercy of the town.

He climbed aboard his buggy. 'I reckon you're right,'

he called back to Kenna. With that he gave the reins a flick and headed out, taking care not to appear to be in any particular hurry. 'Damn fools the lot of them,' he muttered beneath his breath.

Turning his head for a last look at the town, he saw Reverend Dent staring after him. There was a speculative look in Dent's eyes that he did not much care for. But maybe there was something in his own expression that warned the man to keep his lips buttoned, for Dent turned away without saying a word.

No doubt he would voice his suspicions once Luther was well clear of the town.

'Well, Miz Timberlee, you might as well join me in the front seat,' he drawled once he'd cleared the town.

'Don't you be getting any ideas!' Miz Timberlee, he saw, was a scrawny woman with bright-red hair: the kind that came from a bottle.

'Now I know you're joshing,' Luther muttered, thinking that she did not compare favourably with Maybelle, whose shape, he'd noticed, was mighty pleasing to the eye.

'What the hell do you mean?' Miz Timberlee challenged, for clearly this was not the answer she had been expecting.

Wisely he ignored the question. 'Well, I reckon you can help out with the chores, washing our duds and seeing to our meals. You can make yourself useful until it's safe for you to move on. There's just me and old Clarence and we won't bother you none. We've got matters of importance needing our attention.'

Miz Timberlee restrained an overwhelming urge to box his ears. Luther Larkin, no-account bum that he was, stood between her and a vengeful town. He was her only hope. She dared not rile him.

'Well, I ain't apologizing for what I done, Luther Larkin. That schoolmarm deserved what she got!'

'If you say so, Miz Timberlee, but I can tell you now that I don't give a damn about the pair of you and your foolish falling out. And I reckon Amos Standish won't give a damn either, so we've no need to worry about him turning up at the ranch demanding that I hand you over.'

'Standish might not give a damn but there will be others that will,' she warned.

He knew darn well she was right. If he protected Miz Timberlee there'd be folk out to do him harm. But he found he did not give a damn about that either. Hell, maybe he was on the way to turning into a killer. He sure hoped folk would let him be, but if not he was ready. Nor was he going to skulk out at his ranch. He'd return to town whenever he damn well pleased, for it was important they knew he was not running scared.

Sheriff Amos Standish punched the air with his fist. He was in his office reading the news and he had just read that Warden Comfrey was missing. Sure as hell that crazy murdering varmint Ambrose Penrose would have had something to do with the missing warden.

Clear as day, Larkin was nothing but trouble.

The door of the jailhouse burst open and, panting with excitement, Reverend Dent burst in. Perspiration dripped from his nose.

'Larkin!' he wheezed flearly out of breath.

'What's he done now?'

'Nothing yet but he is at the saloon, bold as you please.'

'What's that to me? I've made it plain I'm not making a fool of myself hunting down a runaway floozie. Fact is she saved me a heap of trouble by getting out of town.'

'Arthur Blunt is on his way to the saloon and he's carrying his bullwhip. He aims to use it. He says he knows Larkin sneaked that floozie out of town. He says he knows that woman is hiding out with Luther Larkin. He says if you ain't going to do anything about it he will!' Dent paused, then went on. 'What are you going to do about Arthur Blunt?'

The lawman hesitated. Larkin ought not have facilitated the breakout at the penitentiary! 'Not a damn thing. I'm not of a mind to save Luther Larkin from the whipping he deserves.'

'But you're the law!'

'I'll be along presently. I have some paperwork needing my attention. But if you want to play the peacemaker you have my blessing.'

Dent slunk out of the jailhouse without another word.

Standish knew that Larkin's hide would take a shredding. Blunt was real handy when it came to cracking a whip. He was capable of near breaking a man's wrist when a man tried to haul iron. Blunt's whip was made of hippo hide.

The lawman sighed. Dent was the one who had told the town where Miz Timberlee was hiding out.

'I've been looking for you. And here you are. You no-account varmint!' Arthur Blunt burst through the batwings.

Luther did not turn his head immediately. Carefully he put down his tankard of tepid beer. He'd come into town for a beer, believing it important to make it clear that he was not hiding out: not quaking in his boots in case a posse showed up at his door intent upon taking Miz Timberlee. These townfolk must recognize that they were not going to be able to wipe their boots on him.

'The whole town knows you have that no-account woman Timberlee hiding out at your place,' Blunt accused. 'And now I'm going to teach you a lesson you'll never forget. I'll learn you to meddle in matters that ain't your concern.'

'Who put you up to this?' It was a hunch, but from the shifty look that spread across Blunt's face Luther knew he'd guessed right. This was not Blunt's own idea.

As expected, Blunt ignored the question. 'You think you can haul out that Peacemaker and bring me down, well you think wrong.'

'Lord's sake, one of you men fetch the sheriff,' a saloon woman cried. Luther saw that the long-haired barman had a tight grip on the woman's arm. There was a feral expression on the man's face. Clearly the galoot was siding with Arthur Blunt.

'Mind your manners, woman,' the man snarled.

'Back away, man. It's not too late,' Luther urged. But, even as he spoke he knew he was wasting his breath.

'Are you ready for what's coming your way?' Blunt jeered. He spat and the gob of yellow spittle landed on the toe of Luther's boot. 'That critter would be on her way to an asylum if it weren't for you, Luther Larkin. Yes sir, Doc went and certified her. She is deranged. No sane woman would have done what she did.'

'And she's a damn thief!' the barkeeper accused.

'Helped herself from the till before she took off!'

'Are you acquainted with hippo hide? I guess you must have had a good few whippings during your time inside,' Blunt taunted.

'If he ain't acquainted he sure as hell will be,' the barkeeper joked.

If the show didn't go as planned the fool of a barkeeper would reach for the shotgun squirrelled away beneath the bar, Luther thought. And it would not be Arthur Blunt who would be blown in two.

Clear as day, Standish must by now have been told what was going on at the saloon. It seemed the lawman did not give a damn. And that was just too bad for Arthur Blunt.

'You've done this before,' Luther essayed, wondering how many of the big man's victims had fully recovered after the ordeal.

Three men had followed on close behind Blunt. Maybe they were sidekicks. Maybe they intended to join in, using their boots to finish the job of destroying Luther Larkin.

Blunt guffawed. His expression was jovial. 'Any last words? Who knows? Lick my boots and you may escape a licking.' He guffawed again. But Luther wasn't listening. The time for talking was over. He moved fast.

The barkeeper, licking his lips in anticipation, was caught by surprise as Luther Larkin's elbow connected with the bony structure of his fleshy nose. As the man howled and reached for his nose Luther vaulted the bar. Blunt, reacting quickly, raised his arm, brought the whip back, then sent it cracking across the bar. But Luther was no longer there. Dropping to his knees he made a grab for the concealed shotgun, brought it up butt first, smashing the butt against the barman's skull and reversing the weapon just as Blunt swung back his arm in readiness for another blow.

From behind the bar he brought the shotgun to bear upon the stupefied spectators. Grins that had been spread across eager faces were slipping now as folk realized that the tables had been turned.

Arthur Blunt, unable to stop the momentum of his arm, brought the whip down for a lethal strike just as Luther, realizing he had no choice, pulled the trigger. Blunt was cut near in two by the blast.

'Well, it ain't such a joke now, is it?' Luther yelled. On the floor the barkeeper groaned and Luther, fuelled by righteous rage, bestowed a vicious kick.

'Goddamn it, Larkin, you've killed Arthur Blunt,' a waddy accused as though Luther was the one responsible for the fracas. 'And what the hell have you done to Silas?'

'I wouldn't be surprised if Silas's head ain't busted,' a saloon woman observed cheerfully.

'Some folk just can't be trusted to tend to their own affairs. And that Goddamn barkeeper was one of them.'

Amos Standish regarded his mug of coffee. This morning his wife had given him hell. According to her, if he were any kind of a decent lawman he would have ridden out to the old Grainger spread and taken Miz Timberlee into custody.

'Why, respectable women are afraid to walk the side-walks. That creature has set a precedent,' his wife had griped. It had been no use telling her that Timberlee knew better than ever to show her face in town again.

The jailhouse door burst open and Dent tumbled in. 'You've left it too late. Luther Larkin has shot and killed

Arthur Blunt,' he accused.

Amos Standish suddenly realized he'd made an error of judgement. He had to be seen to be in charge of the town. Now he'd be accused of being afraid to face Larkin. Folk in this town liked to point the finger. Grabbing his shotgun he headed for the saloon:.

'Show's over folks!' he announced as he entered the saloon. 'This place is closed for the rest of the day. Get along, go home; get about your business. Do you hear me?' He raised his voice but they just stood gawking as if unable to believe what they had witnessed.

'You sure as hell took your time getting here,' Luther accused. 'It appears to me you wanted Blunt to cut me to shreds. Did it never occur to you that I would be forced to defend myself! And now a man has died for nothing! Who the hell cares if two fool women fall out over a piece of sidewalk?'

'Get the hell out of my town,' Standish snarled. He knew Luther was damn right.

Larkin's lips twisted. He retrieved Blunt's whip. 'I guess he won't need this. I'll keep it as reminder of a lawman who chose not to uphold the law!'

'This ain't a carnival! Get!' The lawman rounded on the spectators.

'I thought it was,' Luther smiled bitterly. 'You think on this, lawman: if you hadn't railroaded me all those years back I wouldn't have been in the state penitentiary in the first place. Don't think I've forgotten you forcing my head into a pail of slops.'

'I thought you were guilty,' Standish retorted, unable to believe he was actually trying to defend his actions.

'Hell, Sheriff, you ought to run him out of town, that's what you ought to do.' The town barber spoke from beyond the batwings. Luther remembered the galoot from years back. The fellow had been on the jury that had convicted him.

'I ain't the kid whose head you held down in the slop bucket,' Luther spoke softly. 'I've broken no laws. And if this town aims to get rid of me they must be prepared to pay the price first. Seeing as I don't count womenfolk any less than men I sure as hell would aim to treat my enemies equally.'

'You damn varmint. Get the hell out of my town.'

'With pleasure,' Luther moved cautiously towards the batwings.

'You're an awkward son of a bitch,' the lawman snarled. 'And keep that woman out of my town.' Standish was determined to have the last word. He followed Larkin out on to the sidewalk and ran into trouble of a different kind.

'It's your duty, Sheriff Standish, your duty to apprehend that woman.' The speaker was the reverend's wife. With her was Mrs Robins.

'Why, anyone would think you were afraid of him.' Mrs Robins pointed at Luther, pinching her thin nose with disgust.

Luther swung into the saddle. 'Hell, anyone would think you females want to see more bloodshed.'

'Are you just going to let him leave, Amos Standish?' The lawman recognized the voice. His wife, her face red and angry, was headed towards him. 'Why, Amos Standish, anyone would think Mrs Robins is correct in naming you a coward.'

At that Standish snapped. He drew back his hand and

struck his wife across the face. 'Since when have you been sheriff of this town, woman? There ain't no one in this town got the right to tell me how to do my job, and that includes you.' He stormed away, unable to trust himself around Mrs Standish. Hell, now he'd be a laughing stock.

'Hold up there, Luther Larkin.' The saloon woman lounging outside the livery barn stepped into the street. She gave him a wink. He neither winked nor smiled back.

'I ain't going to bite you. I'm a friend of Miz Timberlee.'

'She's doing fine. Ain't much of a cook but . . .' he shrugged. There was no point in bad-mouthing Miz Timberlee.

'Well what do you expect? Cooking ain't her forte! I'm Miz Ruby, by the way.'

'If you have something to say, Miz Ruby, spit it out. I've no interest in idle talk.'

'Well, ain't you a friendly one,' she retorted quickly. She lowered her voice. 'Now keep it under your hat, but Marcus Cooper is sending for Donald Ricket. Heard of him, have you?'

'The gunfighter?'

'Yep. That's him.'

'So how do you know this, Miz Ruby?'

'I know plenty. Drunks always blab. Do you think you're any match for Ricket?'

'What do you care?'

'I don't. Just want to know which one of you to bet on.'

'Well, I aim to keep breathing, if that's any help.'

'Want to know who gave Arthur Blunt the idea of giving you a whipping? Ain't you interested in knowing?'

'Higgy Shaw.' He made a guess.

'Don't be a fool. Do you think Arthur Blunt would give Higgy Shaw the time of day?'

'Who was it then?'

'Why, Miz Maybelle Cooper, that's who.' With that, shrugging her shoulders and swinging her hips, Miz Ruby sauntered away leaving Luther dumfounded.

He could not believe what she'd said. True, she had no reason to lie. But nor had Miz Maybelle any reason to do him harm, unless loyalty to Marcus played a part in her reasoning. If it were true, then that fool Blunt was dead on account of Maybelle's sweet smile.

Ambrose Penrose had often warned that where womenfolk were concerned there was just no telling what they were liable to do.

Had he been wrong about her all along? Was she capable of killing Hamish Cooper? Somehow he did not think she was, but on reflection she was probably capable of getting someone to do the killing for her. Maybe she was even behind Marcus's decision to hire Donald Ricket.

Hardly aware of what he was doing he headed for the white-fenced cemetery that lay just beyond the town boundaries. Now his pa had been a no-account drunk, who had not said one word in defence of his son, nor even visited whilst Luther had been incarcerated. The fact was that, as time went by, Luther had forgotten about his old man.

'Hell I don't know what I'm even doing here,' he mumbled to himself. But this wasn't quite true. He needed time for the anger that raged inside to settle and cool before he rode back to the ranch. He felt like a volcano ready to explode and that was a dangerous state to be in.

When emotions ran high mistakes were made. He'd learned that lesson whilst in the penitentiary.

Methodically he checked the markers, searching for his pa's name. He didn't find one and that was odd, for he remembered his pa handing over cash to Crisp the undertaker to pay for a burial plot and marker.

'Leastways you'll be able to do the necessary,' Pa had joshed, adding, 'Better with you than me, for every last cent will go on rot-gut liquor. I reckon I ain't got long for this world and I want a respectable send off,' Pa had bleated, doubtless without realizing that his words were prophetic.

So where the hell was Pa? Not in the Black Bear cemetery, that was for sure. That meant that that no-account varmint Crisp had pocketed the coins and planted Pa out in the scrubland normally reserved for those who had died without sufficient coin in their pocket. It was common knowledge in town that travelling bums had to make do with rocks and scrub, for the cemetery was there to serve decent folk.

'If I ain't paid I don't dig,' Crisp told all intending customers.

Now it looked as though even if he were paid he did not always dig, confident in the knowledge that no one in this two-bit town gave a damn, just so long as respectable folk got their plot and marker. Folk in town would have known that Pa had paid, for he had boasted of it often enough.

Luther resolved to have words with Crisp, but not yet. Right now he did not trust himself to go anywhere near the man without throttling him.

Clearly Crisp had not thought that Luther would come home from the state penitentiary and, as no one else in town had clearly given a damn about Luther's pa, Crisp had cheated the dead man out of his box and marker.

'I guess there ain't nothing left of you but a few chewed bones,' Luther muttered as he rode away from the cemetery.

Maybelle Cooper, who had been taking tea at Slim's eating house, moved slowly along the sidewalk. The sheet-wrapped body of a man was being carried from the saloon. Word had reached the restaurant that Luther Larkin had blasted Arthur whilst Sheriff Amos Standish, who had turned chicken, had been holed up in his office.

Maybelle realized that she had considerably underestimated Luther Larkin. So had Marcus! Now a man must be dispatched to hire the notorious killer Donald Ricket. Both she and Marcus begrudged the cost of getting rid of Luther.

She still did not know why Walt had confessed to killing Hamish. Indeed she suspected Walt of lying. But with her brother now dead she guessed she'd never know the truth.

She'd deliberately left Hamish waiting by the creek that day. Maybe Luther Larkin, angry that she had refused his invite to the town picnic, had actually killed Hamish. But he had not seemed angry when she turned him down.

Amos Standish blocked her way, his face red and angry.

'You tell your husband, Miz Cooper, that this is my town. We've had enough killing, I say. You tell him that if any hired gunman shows up in my town he'll have me to deal with. And that goes for him too. Folk hereabouts need reminding that no one is above the law. Do you hear me?'

CHAPTER 5

Donald Ricket was clearly a man who liked to impress. Apart from his silver satin waistcoat his garb was black and his eyes were cold! They were the eyes of a killer, of a man who was proud of what he did.

Sam, the waddy dispatched by Marcus Cooper to engage Ricket's services, had been reduced to stuttering beneath that cold gaze. He knew he had sounded as though he were begging Ricket to take the job.

'Business has never been better,' Ricket declared. He had listened as Sam repeated word for word Rancher Marcus Cooper's offer of employ. 'And folk generally come in person. But your boss has chosen to send a hireling. Why is that, do you think?'

'I just do what the boss tells me,' Sam stuttered, knowing he was in dangerous waters.

'Your boss might need me but sure as hell I don't need him.' Ricket smirked. 'I've more business coming my way than I can handle, with land disputes erupting throughout the territory. It's these damn pesky settlers, they need putting in their place.'

'Yes sir,' Sam agreed respectfully. He was no fool and knew that behind Ricket's smile danger lurked.

Ricket had come a long way from being an orphaned boy shipped West to be used as a virtual slave by a no-account lazy bum of a sodbuster. He'd never forget that first winter. They'd been snowed in real bad and the farmer and his wife had taken to keeping him short of food, taking near every morsel for themselves.

He'd known he was not going to get through that winter unless he took drastic action. There hadn't been any other way. He'd waited until the pair had been asleep, then he'd snuck up on them. He remembered the way he'd swung the axe, bringing it down with sickening thuds. It really hadn't been personal. He'd had the fore-sight to realize that this winter was going to be one of the worst. Food was short. He had not wanted to starve to death.

Events had proved that he had made the right decision. The supplies stored by the feckless sodbusters were insuf-ficient. Alive they were no damn use. Dead, at least they had kept him from starving. He had cooked up his meat and a few mouldering potatoes and got through that winter. When the thaw came, well there wasn't much to be planted, just stripped bones that he'd planted deep. Just in time, for sure enough, by and by a neighbour had swung by to check on the feckless pair. Finding them long gone he had taken the bawling distraught boy into town.

There he'd stayed, sleeping back of the saloon, clean-ing spittoons and mopping up stained sawdust. It had not been long before the travelling gunmen who passed through town had become his heroes. He saw with awe the respect these men generated and knew that he wanted it for himself.

Well, now he had it. Except it seemed that this rancher, Marcus Cooper, seemed to think it was just fine to send along a hired man.

It placated him somewhat to observe that the man dispatched by Cooper stood rigidly to attention in front of the table. Ricket had deliberately not invited the man to sit. It pleased the gunman that this one was astute enough to realize men didn't sit at his table unless invited. He'd killed men out of hand for less.

Sam swallowed and shifted uncomfortably beneath the gaze of the killer's cold eyes. The gunman reminded him of a snake getting ready to strike.

'Cooper might be your boss,' Ricket explained with elaborate patience, 'but he sure as hell ain't mine. The fact of the matter is, everyone wants a piece of Donald Ricket. There just ain't enough pieces to go round. I'm being overloaded with requests to help out. Do you understand my predicament?'

'Yes sir, I reckon I do, Mr Ricket!'

'So rather than turn away those in need I hit upon the idea of setting up as an expediter. That means that I give my word: my word, you understand?'

Sam who didn't quite understand, nodded.

'That the matter will be satisfactorily taken care of but not necessarily by me,' Ricket continued. 'Plainly speaking, that means I handle the challenging assignments and what I call the dross I contract out to less experienced galoots, thereby giving them a taste of the pie. Are you following me?'

'Yes sir.'

'Good. I don't much care for galoots who choose to argue.' The gunman paused before continuing: 'Now this Luther Larkin, from what you've told me comes under the heading of dross. One of my hirelings can deal with him. If in the unlikely event that this hireling messes up and gets himself killed I myself will head for Black Bear Crossing to give Luther Larkin my personal attention. As I've told you, cowpoke, once money crosses this table the target is a dead man walking. You have my word on that. My word's good enough for you, ain't it?'

'Yes sir.' Rapidly Sam placed the wad of bills on the table. He wasn't sure whether he had misread the signs but a hunch told him that a refusal on his part to accept Donald Ricket's word would have been an insult that could not be left unchallenged.

His boss might call him every kind of damn fool and throw whatever object might be at hand at his head, but leastways he'd still be breathing. He'd keep his thoughts to himself, but those thoughts were that Cooper had made one hell of a mistake in hiring this man.

'Wise man.' Ricket pocketed the bills without counting them. Only a damn fool would short-change him. 'Now, get yourself back to this big shot, this Marcus Cooper, and tell him that the matter is in hand.'

'Yes sir.' Sam headed for the batwings but before he reached them a tall lanky young fellow stuck out a leg and sent the cowpoke flying. Laughter broke out as Sam scrambled to his feet and made his escape.

Ricket joined in the laughter. 'Well, Ollie, do you want the job of heading for Black Bear Crossing to dispatch this here Luther Larkin?' he asked.

'Yes, I sure do,' Oliver Lewis, a tall, lanky young fellow, winked. 'Keeping the ladies happy is a damned expensive business,' he joked.

'Well, remember what I've told you. Stay away from rot-gut liquor and women till you have gunned down your target. Both have been the ruination of many a good man.' Loud laughter greeted these words of wisdom.

William Crisp, the undertaker, having heard that Luther Larkin had visited the cemetery, was now living in dread and cursing himself for believing that Larkin would rot and die in the state penitentiary.

He had thought of asking Sheriff Amos Standish for protection just in case Larkin came calling, but Standish was like a bear with a sore head as Mrs Standish refused to have him home. Folk were saying she had behaved like a crazy woman, smashing mirrors and clocks and screeching at Amos.

The town reckoned he had got his just deserts, it being recognized that if a man wanted to hit his wife it should be done in the privacy of the home and not out in public on Main Street.

Crisp's only comfort was that Cooper had gone ahead and sent for the gunman Donald Ricket. Even though Standish was making it clear there would be hell to pay should a hired gun show up in his town. But, in Crisp's opinion and that of many other folk, Ricket could not get here fast enough. It did not matter that the men Larkin had killed had brought misfortune upon themselves because folk were thinking that maybe Larkin might take it into his head to look up the folk who had wronged him all those years ago.

Well, Crisp had never voiced an opinion of Luther's guilt or innocence, but he'd stolen the cash handed over by Luther's pa. He'd denied the man a decent burial. He'd even stolen his boots!

Now, shaking in his own boots, he found himself praying that Larkin would leave him in peace. But when the hammering on his door commenced he knew his prayers had not been answered.

'I'll smash in your goddamn door if you don't answer it!' His stomach lurched as he recognized Larkin's voice.

With a shaking hand he unbolted his door. He wasn't even going to try and make a fight of it. It would do him no damn good considering the kind of man Larkin was these days.

'I've waited awhile before calling round,' Luther stated without preamble. 'I just could not trust myself to be around a man like you!' He paused. 'Well, now I am here. You had best tell me what you have done with my pa's remains!'

'I buried him out on the scrubland,' Crisp quavered.

'Let me guess!' Luther smiled unpleasantly. 'Without even a box to protect his remains should coyotes decide to dig them up. Those you bury out on the scrubland are not planted deep, are they? You don't even plant them at all. Just merely pile a few rocks over the corpse if it's lucky. You denied my pa a decent burial together with a few words from Reverend Dent. You're a low-down thief, Crisp.'

'I didn't think you'd get out of the state penitentiary,' Crisp grizzled. 'And no one in town would have come along to witness the burial. No one even asked what I'd done with him. He was a mean-hearted old drunk and all that came out of his mouth were profanities.'

'Maybe so,' Luther agreed. 'But that don't alter the fact that he'd put enough away for a decent departure. Coin by coin he squirrelled his burial money away.'

'What are you going to do?' Crisp clutched a table for support. He could scarcely stand, so great was his fear.

'Now give me a reason why I shouldn't put a snake in your craw.' To the undertaker's terror Luther held up the gunny sack he'd brought with him. The sack twitched.

'I'll pay you back more than he gave,' Crisp screamed.

'That's what I wanted to hear. Now I'm warning you, Crisp, that although I am allowing you to buy your way out of trouble there are some who won't. Next time you are of a mind to dump a man out in the scrub you think long and hard about such a foolhardy step. I've thought things through and what you done to my pa ain't worth killing you over, but next time someone comes calling you might not escape lightly.'

Crisp nodded. 'I know I did wrong,' he pleaded desperately. 'I know I cheated your pa out of a marker and a few comforting words.'

'Did you take his clothes as well? I've heard tell you even sell the duds you've taken from the dead.'

'Times are hard,' Crisp bleated, reminding Luther of a sheep. 'The dead don't need their possessions. No, I did not take your pa's duds. No one would have wanted them in any event.' He paused. 'All I've done is helped folk in need,' Crisp continued to defend himself. 'Those down on their luck ain't particular where their duds come from.

Now here, take this. I've kept the journal wrote by Walt Grainger himself. The last entry made was the day after Hamish was killed. Maybe you'd care to know why Walt killed Hamish.'

'Don't you know? You must have read it.'

'Well, it is in some kind of code old Walt must have devised. I ain't had time to decipher it.'

Luther took the journal without much interest. He shoved it into his back pocket after flicking through the pages which, he noted, were indeed coded. If he were to learn that either Marcus or Maybelle were behind the killing of his pa he would not be surprised.

Marcus Cooper sat behind his mahogany desk, his boots scuffing the polished wood. He removed a cheroot from between his lips and stubbed it viciously against the wood.

He'd been slighted by a no-account gunman.

Hell, he wished he was stubbing the cigar into Ricket's eye.

'I had to go along with him, boss,' Sam bleated, 'for I could see he would have gunned me down had I dis-agreed.'

'Get out of my sight. I ought to have known better than to rely on you to negotiate with a man such as Ricket! Doubtless you were quaking in your boots.'

'Well, I won't deny that I was. He put me in mind of a cat amusing itself with a mouse,' Sam blustered.

'And draw your pay. I don't want to see your miserable face on my property.'

Wisely, Sam knew better than to argue. Without a word he began to retreat backwards towards the door. Cooper's resolve snapped. He picked up a heavy glass paperweight and hurled it at the young waddy and was somewhat surprised that Sam's reaction was up to scratch. The waddy ducked and the paperweight thudded against the door. Then Sam was gone, which was smart for Cooper's hand was closing over the butt of his Peacemaker.

Ricket was too damn big for his boots. He was nothing but a hireling. Cooper would have liked to tell Ricket to go to hell, but that fool Sam had handed over the cash. Now presumably a second-rate hired gun was on his way to deal with Larkin.

Maybelle Cooper came into the room. She'd heard it all anyway as she had been listening at the keyhole. He poured them both a generous measure of whiskey.

'We're going to have trouble with Sheriff Standish,' she warned. 'The man has become obsessed with keeping his reputation as an honest lawman. Why, last time I was in town he made a point of telling me to let you know he could not be bought for he had turned a blind eye long enough.' She poured another generous measure before continuing, 'I've been thinking of how best to deal with him. And I've hit upon an excellent means of ensuring the man does not stick his nose into our concerns.'

'What the hell has got into the man? I know he has no time for Larkin, for he blamed Larkin for the jail breakout. They have got them all except that crazy killer Ambrose Penrose. Well, that man will know better than to show his nose in my town!'

Maybelle nodded, 'Domestic matters are at the root of why Amos Standish is now starting to throw his weight around. I think he is hoping that Luther will tire of playing two-bit rancher and head on out under his own steam as long as he ain't challenged in any way. He says if you just ignore the man he'll drift away like the tumble-weed.'

Marcus shrugged, 'Too late for that, my dear, for Ricket's man is on his way. Just as well, for I reckon it is going to be another long hot summer. Without access to the Big Muddy I can think of two ranchers who will go under, that's for sure. I need that land and I need it now. If I'm going to launch into politics I must be seen to be a cattle baron, not just another frontier rancher. With hind-sight I can see that my biggest mistake was not dealing with Walt before he made his deathbed confession. Why'd he do it! Any idea?'

'None. For all I know he might even have killed your brother. Or he might even have brought Luther back here deliberately to be a burr in your side, for he never much cared for you!'

Cooper smiled unpleasantly, 'My bets are still on you, Maybelle.'

Miz Timberlee lit a cheroot as she watched Luther practise his shooting. 'You're not fast enough,' she drawled. 'I've seen Donald Ricket haul iron and you are not his match. You will not be able to best him. You're as good as dead if you face him man to man out on Main Street.'

'Well that ain't likely, Miz Timberlee, as word is he's not coming to town himself, me not being worth his personal attention.'

She shrugged, 'You still won't be good enough whoever turns up. You just ain't had enough time. Although I'd say you are showing promise.'

'Well, thank you very much for that, Miz Timberlee! And why might you be concerned?'

'Well it ain't on account of you, Luther Larkin. We both know there are still folk in that town looking to have me committed as a mad woman. Only the fact that you proved yourself a killer has kept them from hammering at your door. I'm also saying that there ain't no need for you to play fair and square. I'm willing to help you out.'

'What the hell do you mean? How can you help out?'

With a shrug of her shoulders she told him, concluding with a smirk, 'Clarence ain't much use to you in these circumstances. The old coot has still got the shakes. Rot-gut liquor ain't worked itself out of his system. And won't for some considerable time.'

'What you're proposing to do ain't a womanly thing to do, Miz Timberlee. Why, the town would lynch you if they caught you. Besides which I'm hoping it won't be necessary. Amos Standish has made it plain he will not countenance hired guns in his town. As far as I've heard neither Donald Ricket nor his men have ever openly gunned down a lawman. They know damn well that would be crossing the line and liable to stir up a hornet's nest.'

'You're a fool to rely on Amos Standish for help. He turned a blind eye when Arthur Blunt aimed to set about you!' She laughed. 'You're a fool to think Marcus Cooper has not taken Standish's presence into consideration. He'll have plans for the lawman, that's for sure.'

'Even if you deal with Ricket's man it will not be the end of matters.' declared Clarence, who had been listening to the exchange. 'Fact is, I'd say it would be the beginning.'

'Why's that?'

'Well, ain't it obvious? Ricket will be obliged to clear up the mess himself. He was the one who took Cooper's cash. He'll come to town with a veritable army to hunt you down and see you dead. His reputation would be at stake.' The old man shook his head. 'I'm gonna assume that you aren't looking to die out on Main Street.'

'Well, you assume right!'

'Well then, you're obliged to accept Miz Timberlee's mighty generous offer to even the odds.'

'But it don't seem right. She is a woman, after all. It's an underhand way of going about matters.'

'Hell. Luther Larkin, ain't life in the state penitentiary taught you any sense?' Clarence did not wait for a response. 'After we've dealt with Ricket's man we must hightail it out and find a place of our choosing to deal with whoever comes to hunt us down. I know such a place, but we won't talk on that now.'

'He's right, Luther. This town will not let you be!'

Luther was inclined to agree. 'If you'll excuse me, Miz Timberlee, I aim to get on with my shooting practice.'

She shook her head. 'You still won't be able to deal with any hired killer fair and square. Why do you think Ricket is sending one of his hirelings? It is because he thinks you ain't worth a spit. By dying out on Main Street all you will do is prove him right.'

CHAPTER 6

Unlit cheroot clamped between his teeth, Sheriff Amos Standish lounged against the jailhouse door. Mrs Standish was still acting crazy and refusing to let him home, but right now he had Marcus Cooper and his hired gun to think about. He'd be forced to haul iron, no doubt about it.

He frowned as he spotted storekeeper Kenna heading his way. The man saw himself as the eyes and ears of the town. In fact the lawman liked to joke that Kenna would have made a better lawman than he did. The man's gimlet eye missed nothing.

Whatever the news might be, Standish knew it would not be to his liking.

'A young gunman calling himself Oliver Lewis has put up at the Cooper ranch,' Kenna announced, 'We don't want gunfighters in our town. I've seen what they can do when they take over a town. Innocent folk get hurt.'

'Quit fretting. If Lewis shows his nose in my town he's a dead man, for I have made it plain I am not having guns for hire in my town. The day I cannot handle young upstarts like Lewis is the day I will take off my star, and I've no intention of doing that yet awhile.'

So Marcus Cooper had brought in a hired gun despite being warned that no one was above the law. Well, that was a goddamn mistake if ever there was one. He'd throw Cooper into jail for this and leave him to sweat awhile.

Across Main Street Maybelle Cooper drove into town apparently going in the direction of Slim's eating house. He ignored her. The time for talking was done. The Coopers would soon learn that this was his town. His word was law.

'We don't often see you in here, Mrs Cooper.' Slim, wiping his hands on his greasy apron, waddled out from behind his counter to greet the rancher's wife.

'Have Dolly bring me over a pot of tea,' she ordered and settled herself down to wait for Dolly, the ancient waitress. When Dolly shuffled over she invited her to sit, knowing that Slim would not dare interrupt. No one in this town dared disrespect Mrs Maybelle Cooper.

She lowered her voice, 'I've a deal to put to you, Dolly. I know you are a woman I can trust. I'm going to give you the means to get out of town in return for a small favour.'

Dolly's eyes widened as she listened without interruption. Then she smiled. 'God bless you, Mrs Cooper. You can count on me, for I detest this town.'

The two women smiled at each other as an envelope filled with a wad of cash changed hands beneath the cover of Slim's none too clean tablecloth.

'Get on with your work,' Slim snarled once Mrs Cooper had left the restaurant. 'Do you hear me, you old bag of bones? You must have been mighty pretty once, like Mrs

Cooper,' he jibed, 'And now look at you, You're as ugly as sin. And that's a fact.'

She didn't answer. Tomorrow was a new day. And for one galoot in particular it was going to be his last day. She didn't particularly dislike Amos Standish but Slim – well, he was another matter entirely. And now he'd overstepped the line one time too many!

Upon learning the arrangement that Maybelle had made with Dolly, Marcus scowled at his wife. 'We've wasted good money. Slim would have done it. For nothing! The man's a craven coward. It wouldn't take much to twist his arm!'

'Eventually he would have blabbed. The man's a coward, I agree. He is also a man who cannot hold his liquor. Now Dolly will keep her mouth shut. No one will even miss her until she is long gone.'

Whistling cheerfully Oliver Lewis the gunman rode into town. He had been assured by Rancher Cooper that he need not concern himself about the town's lawman, Amos Standish. He rode slowly down the dusty main street and tethered his horse outside the saloon. Folk were gawking at him. They knew who he was. Word had spread. They knew why he was here, and they were fearful lest he turn his attention to them.

'Hey kid.' He snapped his fingers at the red-headed youngster who was openly staring, mouth agawp. He took a wad of bills from his pocket and peeled off a note. 'Want to earn some cash?'

The kid nodded vigorously.

'Then take this missive to Luther Larkin. Tell him that

I'm ready on his pleasure. And that if he does not show up then we'll all know him for the yellow-belly he is.'

The kid snatched the money and the missive.

Oliver Lewis strolled into the saloon where he intended to hold court whilst he waited for Larkin. Cooper had assured him that the man would take up the challenge.

The barkeeper, who had been about to ask the young killer to pay for his beer, suddenly thought better of it. Lewis's kind took umbrage mighty easily.

'You had better watch out, mister,' an oldster observed, 'For Amos Standish, our lawman, has no liking for hired guns!'

'Ain't you heard? Your lawman is laid low with food poisoning. He could be dead for all I know and care.'

Miz Ruby, who had been lounging against the door, abruptly headed for the batwings.

'You're fired. I ain't having you back,' the barkeeper bellowed. 'You can set yourself up in a shack on the outskirts of town with all the other old crones. You're getting long in the tooth and that's a fact.'

Ruby paused on the sidewalk. She was surprised to see Dolly from the restaurant about to board the eastbound stage. The restaurant, she noticed, was closed.

She stepped towards the stage, wanting to speak to Dolly but was too late, for, with an ear-splitting whoop the driver cracked his whip and the stage surged forward. Ruby frowned and broke into a run. Now she knew something was wrong. There'd been a furtive look about Dolly that had aroused her suspicions. Since Standish had been kicked out by his wife all his meals had come from Slim's restaurant.

'You're a wretched sight in the light of day,' a voice jeered.

Miz Ruby didn't stop to think. She lashed out, but Higgy, moving with surprising speed managed to avoid her hand.

'You ain't a paying customer now, Higgy, and if I get my hands on you I can guarantee you won't be smiling.'

'You washed-out old floozie,' he yelled as he backed away. But she had no time for the snivelling coward. Instinct told her something was wrong. Then she saw an ashen-faced Kenna leaving the jail.

'Fetch the doc,' he yelled. 'It's Sheriff Standish. He's been taken real bad.'

'I'll tell his wife.' Higgy was in his element. 'She'll want to know.'

Ruby waited on the sidewalk. She wanted to rush and help the lawman but for now all she could do was watch developments. After all, Mrs Standish would be on her way. She watched as Doc came hurrying down Main Street. Higgy was back also, but without Mrs Standish.

'She ain't coming. She says he can rot for all she cares,' Higgy told anyone who would listen before turning his attention once again to Ruby. 'Someone ought to dump that floozie in the horse trough. She's wearing too much war paint,' he yelled, and to her disbelief a couple of farmers, encouraged by their wives, grabbed her. Before she realized what they were about she was dumped in the trough.

'What the hell is going on here;' a voice yelled as Doc Grimes and Kenna emerged from the jailhouse. 'Show some respect. Your lawman is close to death and all you can do is horse around. You there!' he pointed at Ruby, 'If you want to be of use tend the sheriff.' Rapidly he issued instructions.

A man walked on to the street. Folk parted to let him through, for it was the young gunman.

'I say let him be,' Lewis declared. 'And that goes for all of you. Do you understand!' He tapped the butt of his Peacemaker. From their expressions he saw that they did indeed understand his meaning.

'Well, it don't go for me!' Ruby glared at him. 'And if you are not happy with that I'll strap on a Peacemaker and we'll settle the matter. Let me tell you, mister, I ain't scared of you.'

Lewis laughed. 'Well, you can do as you please. Most women do in the end. But in the event of the lawman breathing his last you come on over to the saloon and keep me company, for you will find I am pleasant company.'

Ignoring him Ruby entered the jail. She knew she would be the only one tending Amos Standish, for the rest of the folk in this two-bit town were running scared. She could see it in their eyes. Even Doc was unsure whether his position would keep him safe if Oliver Lewis decided to turn vicious.

From the cell where he lay Amos Standish groaned. Miz Ruby shook her head. 'You had better pull through, Amos Standish, for I don't want you dying on me.'

After the kid had departed Luther eyed Miz Timberlee. 'It seems I must accept your offer, seeing as neither of you rate me fast enough to win fair and square. But how the hell you are gonna be able to sneak into town unseen I don't know.'

She smiled, 'Well, it seems folk have forgotten about me for the time being. If I am challenged I'll talk my way out of trouble. Although why we cannot make a run for it now I don't know.'

'Hell, Miz Timberlee, we can't have folk pegging us as cowards!' Clarence exclaimed. 'Such slurs stick. Life is hard enough out here without any worthless bum thinking he can call the shots.'

'Well, I guess Amos Standish has been taken care of, as it seems no-account bums are calling the shots in Black Bear Crossing,' Luther observed.

'Well, he ought to have stamped down hard on Marcus Cooper,' Clarence grumbled.

Higgy Shaw had never felt so good. The gunman Oliver Lewis had bought him a drink. Or at least had ordered Silas, the barkeeper, to give him a drink. Plenty of free drinks were being handed over but Silas was afraid to complain.

The kid, Tommy Kelly, had returned with the message from Larkin that he was to be expected at noon, at which Lewis had declared with good humour that he was perfectly content to wait awhile. Higgy had noticed that although the gunman was 'buying' for the rest of them he himself was not drinking liquor.

Bets were being taken as to whether Larkin would indeed come to town. But no one was betting on the result if the man did show up. There was no way Larkin could beat Ollie Lewis.

Now Higgy was keeping a watch out on Main Street, for noon, the time of the shoot-out, was fast approaching. Spotting a stray dog regarding him with undisguised curiosity, Higgy took up a stone, which he hurled with surprising accuracy. With a yelp the dog limped away. It was then that Higgy thought he detected movement from the top of the church bell tower. His suspicions were aroused.

A rider thundered into town, halted before the saloon and yelled that Luther Larkin and the old man were on their way into town.

'Have you seen my boy? Have you seen Tommy?' Mrs Kelly, looking angry, was out on Main Street. 'He was in the saloon but now he ain't!'

'I ain't seen him, ma'am,' Higgy rejoined with a smirk. He thought the kid might have sneaked up to the bell tower to avoid his ma. Maybe he'd throw a fright into the kid. The idea appealed. He'd also get a bird's eye view of the shoot-out when it took place below. He'd spotted Cooper's men squirreling themselves away in alleyways. It seemed the rancher was taking no chances on Luther Larkin escaping from what was coming his way.

'Are you sure of that, Higgy?' she did not trust him.

'I wouldn't lie to you, ma'am.'

'Well, I'd say you lie to everyone else.' Scooping up her skirts she took off down Main Street, still searching for Tommy.

Maybe, just maybe, if a scare were thrown into him, Tommy might tumble down the bell tower steps, maybe even kill himself or break his back. Nothing would give Higgy more delight than being the bearer of bad news. Without even stopping to think of what he was doing he headed for the bell tower.

Timberlee tensed as she heard the laboured breathing of someone coming up the winding stairs of the tower. It was Higgy. She had glimpsed him down on Main Street. She could not understand why he had not raised the alarm, denounced her and let folk know she was up to no good.

There was no point in appealing to his better nature because he had not got one. Higgy found pleasure in the suffering of others. If folk in this town got their hands on her she'd be the one suffering: railroaded and shipped to an asylum would be her fate. The only reason none of them had come looking for her was that they were now too damn scared of Luther Larkin.

There was no point in pleading with him then to keep his mouth shut for once about matters not his concern. Timberlee reached into the sash she wore around her waist and drew out a length of very thin wire of the type used by Kenna for slicing through cheese.

'You're too long in the tooth. Fact is those teeth of yours remind me of a worn-out old nag,' he had jibed just before the confrontation with schoolteacher, Mrs Fenton, had taken place. He was a skunk but that did not make dispatching him any easier.

'No point you hiding, you little varmint,' Higgy stepped out upon the bell tower platform just as shouts broke out below that Luther Larkin was riding into town.

She was a tall woman and that gave her the advantage. Praying that no one was looking up at the bell tower right now and grasping the wire in gloved hands, she brought it down around his throat and tightened the noose before he'd even realized he was in danger. They both went down upon the floor, Higgy kicking and floundering on top of her as she tightened the wire.

Crazed with terror and afraid that Larkin would be shot down and she'd been sent to an ayslum, she found the strength she needed. Thank the Lord he had not been able to slip a finger between his scrawny neck and the cutting wire. That might have saved him, but the varmint had been too damn slow. He'd not been expecting to find that she was the one up here.

As Higgy expired she reflected that folk weren't exactly thinking about her. Not right now.

This morning she'd encountered one of Cooper's men and had bargained her way into town. 'Just want to see Luther Larkin shot down,' she told him. He'd believed her. As she had expected, the varmint had taken advantage and then let her go on her way.

Marcus Cooper had joined Oliver Lewis in the saloon. Maybelle, much to her displeasure, had been told to stay put at the hotel, it not being seemly for his wife to be seen in the saloon.

Well, it seemed that Larkin was not going to make a run for it. He was heading right into the trap being set, for Cooper had posted shooters in alleyways just in case Lewis was not as proficient at hauling iron as he'd been boasting. This he'd kept from Lewis. The man might take the precautions as a personal insult, for gunmen were an unpredictable breed, always looking for an excuse to kill.

'Larkin is out on Main Street, Mr Lewis. And that old coot Clarence has parked himself at the livery barn ready for a quick getaway when Larkin goes down.'

'Smart man!' Lewis yawned. 'Well, now Larkin can wait on me!' he drawled.

'Good luck to you, Mr Lewis,' someone hollered. 'It's time someone rid our town of scum like Luther Larkin.'

'I've no need of luck,' Lewis reprimanded. 'Now I don't cotton to fool talk about luck. We'll have no more of it.'

Silence greeted this announcement.

It suddenly occurred to Nate Marsh, the waddy who had brought the news concerning Luther Larkin being on his way to town that he had seen no sign of Miz Timberlee. He was about to speak up, but thought better of it.

'Now, I'll be in your debt if you let me through,' Miz Timberlee had said and had then added that she always paid her debts. Nate swallowed. Well, he could not be expected to shoot a woman, could he? And she sure had paid her debts. He felt his ears grow red.

'Mr Lewis. . . .' The red-headed kid burst through the batwings, practically stuttering with a excitement.

'Don't trouble me now, boy.'

'But . . .' the kid, intent upon delivering the message, moved forward.

Losing patience the gunman kicked out, knocking the kid's legs from under him. With a howl the kid fell to the floor.

'When a man of standing says not to trouble him you take note. Now there ain't no need to be thanking me for teaching you a lesson that might just save your life one day.'

With that, supremely confident and relishing every moment of being the centre of attention, the gunman made for the batwings.

Tommy Kelly's legs throbbed with pain.

'Well, I darn well won't tell you,' he howled. He'd spotted Miz Timberlee up on the bell tower. He sniffed. No one was paying him any mind. Men crowded to the batwings and windows, all wanting to see Luther Larkin shot down.

Tommy had read everything he could about the hired killers he so much admired. He wanted to be one himself one day. He knew Timberlee was up on the bell tower for a reason. He guessed she could shine a light into Mr Lewis's eyes, so blinding him at the critical moment so that he could not shoot straight. He could have told anyone who would listen that Mr Ricket would come to town if Luther did not die. And then there would be trouble.

As no one was paying him any mind he took up a half-drunk glass and swallowed a mouthful. His legs sure ached and folk had sniggered when he went down.

CHAPTER 7

It's time, Timberlee thought. Her hands were steady although sweat drenched her clothing. She ignored the flies being attracted by the pooled blood beneath Higgy's near-severed head.

Down below she could see Luther Larkin waiting patiently on Main Street. Her sharp eyes caught movement in one of the alleyways.

'Damn it!' she muttered. She was not altogether surprised, for they'd been expecting that Marcus Cooper would not play fair.

Sweat trickled beneath Luther's shoulder blades. He resisted the temptation to look up at the bell tower.

'You think you can come back here and make us eat dirt, Luther Larkin? Well, you can think again,' a voice yelled from somewhere beneath a shuttered window. He recognized the voice as belonging to the barber, and was sure glad he had never dropped in for a shave. And he never would, if he got through this.

Confidently Oliver Lewis swaggered out on to Main Street. He felt invincible. He was important. He was a man to be feared, and above all he liked being able to play God when it came to another man living or dying.

'I sure hope you been saying your prayers!' he called to the man waiting for him out on Main Street. 'Pretty soon you'll be saying howdy to the devil!'

'You're a damn fool,' Luther rejoined. 'Whatever Marcus Cooper has paid you I'd say your life is worth a damn sight more.'

Lewis's jaw gaped open in amazement as he realized the implication of the other man's words. Surely Larkin could not be expecting to walk away from the shoot-out?

'This ain't nothing personal, Larkin, nothing at all,' he replied with a smirk.

'With me it's always personal,' was the unexpected response.

He's trying to rattle me, Ollie thought. *He wants an edge.* He took a deep breath. He knew the importance of calmness before hauling iron. His self-confidence had not been shaken. He was the faster gun. They both knew it.

He smiled as he reached for his Peacemaker. Larkin was reaching also but was a mite slower. Lewis's finger began to tighten on the trigger whilst Larkin was still clearing leather.

Luther knew he was staring death in the face, for the gunman was the faster man. But then the man's head exploded like a shattered melon spraying brains and gore in every direction.

The rifle boomed again and a galoot who had just stepped out of the alleyway went down, blasted near in two by Miz Timberlee.

A bullet whizzed past Luther's ear to bury itself in one

of the sidewalk posts. He spun round and fired at a man emerging from the saloon. The galoot went down, clutching a blasted shoulder.

Inside the saloon the man who had let Miz Timberlee come into town stood as if frozen as he realized what he had done. Well, he never would have thought she was a crack shot, so he was damned if he was shouldering the blame. He'd get as far away from Cooper as he could, and *fast.*

'What the hell is going on? Who the hell has downed Oliver Lewis?' Cooper bellowed.

'Let's get the hell out of here.' Clarence galloped down Main Street with two saddled horses in tow, one for Luther and one for Miz Timberlee.

There was another yell from an alleyway. Another man was down.

Luther swung into the saddle and they galloped down Main Street, then veered to the left, swinging round behind Dent's church just as Miz Timberlee, dressed in bedraggled finery, emerged.

'Let's ride. I've drenched the hymns books in kerosene-and set them afire. I never did care for those hell-fire sermons that Dent liked to deliver!'

Clarence grinned. 'We've sure given this town something to remember, but now we must fork it out, for this ain't over; there's more to come. Let's ride before those polecats find their addled wits.'

But Luther knew this was not exactly true. It was Miz Timberlee who had given the town something to remember. He never would have believed she was such a fine sharpshooter. He also knew the old man was right. The town would not let them be. There'd been slaughter done today in Black Bear Crossing and it did not signify that those slaughtered had only gotten their just deserts.

Tommy Kelly emerged on to Main Street. He rubbed his bruised leg. But he kept his mouth shut, knowing it would not go down well that he'd known about the bell tower.

Everyone was yelling excitedly at once. Marcus Cooper stood alone, a thunderous expression on his face. Then he exploded with rage.

'Goddamn that lazy varmint Ricket to hell,' he yelled. 'That two-bit bum was too damn lazy to get off his butt, so he sends an idiot to do a man's job. The bum is nothing but a cheat.' Cursing, the rancher appropriated Lewis's money belt.

It wouldn't take much to convince townfolk that Walt's confession wasn't worth a spit, even though he'd been dying at the time. He'd just need to get them liquored up.

He fired his Peacemaker into the air to get their attention. 'It's high time this town brought Luther Larkin to justice, for he is a no-account murderer, and I ain't referring to the folk he murdered today.'

'The church is burning. It's going up like tinder.' Kenna rushed down Main Street arms flapping.

'Larkin can wait. We must save the church.' Dent had suddenly found a voice.

To Cooper's umbrage folk seemed to agree with the minister, for they streamed towards the church. He could have told them that they did not have a hope in hell but none of them seemed inclined to listen.

'Dent's right,' Robins declared. 'If the breeze shifts

there a chance other buildings might go up likewise.'

'Too bad, Mr Cooper. It seems you must wait to set off in pursuit of young Larkin,' the ostler observed innocently enough.

Cooper almost attacked the man.

'Well, I must see to my barn.' The ostler departed. He could have said that he had not taken Cooper for a fool and that only a fool would publicly badmouth an egotistical killer such as Donald Ricket. But he'd have been risking his life had he done so.

'You need the town,' Maybelle hissed in her husband's ear. 'Stand them a few drinks and you'll have them following you like the dogs they are!'

'Dump that no-account bum out in the scrub,' Cooper kicked Oliver Lewis's corpse. 'And see to it that my men get the best. Have Dent say a few words as they are planted.' He grabbed hold of the undertaker's black coat. 'And I want them buried with their boots on.' He raised his voice. 'Do you hear me?'

Crisp nodded vigorously. 'I sure do, Mr Cooper. I sure do!' His eyes were straying to the dead gunman's fancy red boots with a white strip of decoration running down each side. Maybe he'd keep them for himself.

Cooper turned to his wife. 'The land is as good as mine.' He managed a grim smile. 'First the county and then the state. It's time to think big. With the Big Muddy in my possession it will not be that difficult to travel from being just another frontier rancher to being an acknowledged cattle baron. I'm aiming high, Maybelle, just as you knew I would. That's why you killed Hamish, wasn't it?'

She smiled. 'Now don't you try pinning that killing on

me. I suspect you killed Hamish on account of my favouring your brother was driving you crazy with jealousy.'

'Have it your way. Who gives a damn?' Together they stood and watched the church burn. 'One way or another Luther Larkin won't be standing in my way. He'll be running for his life, him and that crazy old coot.'

'If you manage to run down Miz Timberlee I suggest you hang her. She deserves it for what she did!'

'Now what are you talking about!'

'You're such a fool, Marcus. Who do you think the sharpshooter was? Who do you think fired the church? It's because of her that your plans came to nothing.'

'No. It's on account of you and other meddling womenfolk. If you women had let Miz Timberlee be she never would have hid out with Luther Larkin. Well, one day, Maybelle Cooper, I might not be around to protect you and your chickens may come home to roost. I'd have been better off wed to Miz Timberlee than you, for leastways she has proved herself mighty handy when it comes to shooting men down. Now we're going home, Mrs Cooper, and when I return to town tomorrow you ain't coming with me.'

Amos Standish peered out of the jailhouse window. He could hardly stand. He was obliged to lean heavily on Miz Ruby. Marcus Cooper, he saw, was headed out and a good many of the townsfolk were riding with him. They were off to make a show of running down Luther Larkin but the lawman doubted whether they would succeed.

A manhunt took determination and stamina. The men riding with Cooper were weaklings, he could see that now.

'Slim's dead, you say?'

'Lucky for you old Dolly didn't bear you any ill will,' Miz Ruby rejoined. 'The Coopers paid her to poison you but you'll never prove it. Dolly's headed East.'

Standish, she observed, looked tired and drawn and now bore no resemblance to the town-tamer he had once been.

'I've had a bellyful of this town – and Mrs Standish,' said the lawman.

'Well, she's coming your way.'

Mrs Standish entered the jailhouse. 'As the Lord has seen fit to spare you I will forgive you. You may return home. And run that creature out of town.' With a sniff she swept out.

'Like I said, I've had a bellyful of Mrs Standish,' the lawman reiterated. 'I'm headed out,' he unexpectedly declared. 'You're welcome to ride along. Stage is leaving today unless I am mistaken.'

'Ain't nothing to keep me here,' Miz Ruby replied.

'We'll stop by the bank. Get ourselves funds and leave town.' He didn't give a damn what befell the town once he left. It was a thankless task being a lawman and he'd had a bellyful. Why, not one person had seen fit to enquire after his health.

At any moment Miz Ruby expected he would change his mind. As they were leaving the bank, they met Kenna on the sidewalk, who declared that it was good to have the lawman back on his feet.

'Well, it's good to be back on my feet,' Amos rejoined. He steered Miz Ruby towards the stage depot, bought two tickets and ushered her into the stage. Across Main Street he spotted a wide eyed Mrs Dent.

'Get moving, stage driver, for I ain't a patient man.' He knew who would be heading down Main Street: his wife, alerted by Mrs Dent.

'I heard tell Rancher Cooper badmouthed Ricket.' The wizened stage driver seemed inclined to linger. 'If that's true, well this town needs a damn good lawman.'

'You're paid to drive the stage. Not to pontificate. Now get moving, I say.'

The stage driver cackled, for he saw a woman running towards the stage. He cracked his whip and the stage lurched forward.

'Get out of the way, you fool woman,' he bawled as the horses picked up speed.

Amos Standish, peering from the stage window, saw his wife tumbling backward. His last view of her was one of her sprawled on the sidewalk, skirt and petticoats in disarray, exposing an unseemly amount of stout leg. He grinned. But Mrs Standish would not be grinning when she realized she'd been left near destitute.

'Word will reach Ricket eventually. Those folk in town were just plain foolish, leaving Ricket's man rotting away out in the scrub. He'll take it as a personal affront. I would have warned them had I believed they would listen. But I knew they would just badmouth me.' Miz Ruby looked at Standish questioningly.

Amos Standish sank back against the upholstery. 'Don't fret yourself, Miz Ruby. Whatever befalls them they brought grief upon themselves.' He shook his head. 'I never would have believed Slim would feed me poison!'

'You ain't much of a lawman, then, Amos for it was old Dolly who fed you poison. And Slim as well, but in his case a far more lethal dose.'

He never would have believed it of Dolly.

'I'm done with Black Bear Crossing,' he reiterated. 'Those folk who rode out with Marcus Cooper, baying for blood, well it seemed they had forgotten there was any law in Black Bear Crossing. Well, they ain't hiding behind my coat tails if trouble comes to town. My town-taming days are done with. Now then, Miz Ruby, just put your mind as to where we might head for. I'll leave it to you.'

'Well I'll be damned.' Ricket recognized the man who had just entered the saloon. He was secretly pleased to see that misfortune had befallen Jethro Fisher. The man had taken a bullet in the leg and and now limped badly.

'I'll buy you a whiskey,' he offered generously. 'But I can't employ a cripple. I was mighty sorry when I heard tell you'd taken a slug in the leg.' He was lying, but what the hell!

'Well, you might also have heard tell that I got my revenge.' Jethro pulled out a chair and sat down! 'I'll take the whiskey.'

Ricket nodded. 'I heard how you burnt out that no-account homesteader, the one who blasted your leg.'

'Yep. He paid for what he did. Damn fool ought to have killed me. Revenge is best served cold. Soon as I was able I paid that varmint a visit.'

'He deserved what he got!' Ricket concurred.

'Too bad he had a family,' Jethro smirked. 'But, like I said, he should have killed me when he had the chance.'

'Damn fool,' Ricket agreed.

The two men drank in companionable silence.

'It's too bad about your man Lewis!' Jethro at last observed.

'What the hell are you talking about?'

'Ain't you wondered why you ain't heard from him? Ain't you wondered how he fared in Black Bear Crossing?'

'Well, it had crossed my mind but these young fighters, well, they like to strike out on their own. I can't blame Ollie for wanting to be as free as the tumbleweed.'

'Then you ain't heard Ollie's head was blasted clean off.'

Ricket whistled. 'Are you saying that two-bit no-account outdrew my man?'

'Nope.'

'Then what are you saying?'

'Larkin had a shooter planted top of the church bell tower. It was a set-up. And Ollie walked right into a trap. He never stood any chance at all. And there is worse!'

'What the hell are you saying?'

'Your man was not even planted decent. Folk just hauled him out into the scrub and left him to rot whilst his bones were picked clean by scavengers. Marcus Cooper ranted and raved, yelling out that you are a no-account bum and that you sent another no-account bum because you were too damn lazy to do the job yourself.'

Ricket nodded, 'And what of Luther Larkin? What did he have to say?'

'Not a damn word. Larkin was not fool enough to stay around, for your man was not the only one to die that day. I believe some of Cooper's men were shot down. Naturally they were buried decent.' Jethro chuckled. 'There was delay in going after Larkin on account of the church going up. But then Cooper riled up the town and set off at the head of a posse, vowing to bring Larkin to justice.'

'And did they?'

'Damn quitters, the lot of them! They never caught up with him. The whole darn bunch of them turned back when it was clear that Larkin was headed out on to the salt flats known as the Devil's Kitchen.'

'Sounds like Cooper's running the town. What about the law?'

'Word is Cooper had the lawman poisoned. When Standish was on his feet he quit and left town.'

'I've heard of Standish. He had quite a reputation as a town-tamer. Too bad we won't get to lock horns. Our kind is a dying breed, Jethro. Why, there are some towns even banning the wearing of Peacemakers within town boundaries.' Slowly Ricket rolled himself a smoke. He was in danger of blasting Jethro. And he was damned if he was going to be the one to put Jethro out of his misery. 'Well, don't let me be keeping you, Jethro. You've given me plenty to think on.'

Jethro Fisher nodded. 'I reckon you have,' he agreed. Ricket's eye was twitching, a sure sign of the man's boiling rage.

'You'll give those varmints their just deserts then. . . .' Jethro hesitated. 'Fact is, I'd be proud to ride with you.'

Ricket shook his head. 'Like I said, I can't use you.' He watched as Fisher limped out.

'I won't give him more than six months,' Ricket said to anyone who cared to listen. 'The day will come when Jethro puts a .45 to his head and blows out his brains. And that is just how it should be. He'll do right. He lives by the gun and he'll die by the gun, but as for Marcus Cooper, I'll have to think up a fitting end for the varmint.'

None of the men who had been lounging around ventured an opinion one way or another. With Ricket it was safest to keep one's lips buttoned, for the man was unpredictably and undoubtedly violently disposed.

'I'll make Marcus Cooper wish he'd never opened his big mouth.'

'Well then maybe I can make a suggestion.' One of the men gave voice at last. 'Way back I hailed from Black Bear Crossing and sure as hell I wouldn't spit on any of them if they were on fire.'

Ricket eyed his man, Fernandez. 'Speak up. Let's hear what you have got to say.'

CHAPTER 8

'Well, I ain't a man to kick a woman out of her home. Mrs Standish can stay.' Cooper chuckled. 'Who would have thought Amos would up and leave along with that no-account floozie.'

And mighty convenient it was. For a riled Amos Standish was not a problem to be lightly dismissed.

'That's fine by me,' Robins rejoined.

'I wasn't asking you.' Marcus Cooper stopped smiling, 'From now on I'm running this town and as long as folk don't step out of line they will find it to be to their advantage.'

'Well, that may be so, with Amos gone.' Robins shrugged. 'Do you reckon Larkin is dead?' he asked casually.

Cooper nodded. 'I expect he is. The fool was headed straight towards the Devil's Kitchen and that's why most of the men voted to give up the chase. I had to agree, much as I wanted to get my hands on the cowardly cur. But I had to accept I could not ask men to venture into the Kitchen. The place is a death trap. I doubt whether Larkin would have made it across. Too bad you did not choose to ride with us.'

'Well, I'm not a well man.'

'From a distance the salt shines like silver. The heat hitting the ground is enough to roast any man fool enough to find himself on foot out in the Kitchen. Folk who get stranded out on the flats go plain crazy and start claiming they can see the devil out there, dancing around as he waits for them to die. Leastways, that is what the rare few who have made it across have been heard to say. Cooper shrugged. 'But who pays attention to crazy folk?'

He fell silent. It would not be wise to reveal that he'd been thinking of taking his younger brother Hamish out into the Kitchen and then leaving him to die. He had even gone so far as to reconnoitre the place. He had ventured a short distance into the Kitchen and had then turned back. It had been like riding into hell. For a moment he had been mortally afraid he would not be able to find his way out of the place.

'Only folk who are crazy try to cross the Devil's Kitchen. I guess Luther Larkin falls into that category. Or maybe he'd sooner face the Kitchen than face me! Now, is there anything else on your mind?'

'As a matter of fact there is. Folk are fretting that maybe Ricket might decide to head our way.'

Cooper forced a smile. 'Ricket follows the cash. He turned down the invite to come to Black Bear Crossing when there was cash to be made. Now that there ain't cash to be made, he won't trouble himself with our two-bit town. But to keep good folk from fretting I aim to place three newly hired men in town. They'll keep the law and run undesirables out.'

Robins realized then that anyone who stood in the way of Cooper's plans to increase his range would be tagged an undesirable and run out of town, if not killed on a pretext.

'Now quit worrying. There will be plenty of work coming your way. Now that I have control of the Big Muddy I aim to expand.'

Unlikely though it might be he would not dismiss the possibility of Ricket putting in an appearance. He'd have lookouts posted around the vicinity of his ranch. The place was well protected, with its own water supply and there was no way Ricket would catch him by surprise in the unlikely event the man was crazy enough to show up.

'And let folk in town know I don't take kindly to criticism,' he concluded warningly.

Miz Timberlee had not stopped griping since they had fled the ranch. She had not wanted to leave. 'Why, I heard tell of a woman driven mad by the sight of the open sky,' she reiterated once again.

'Well, it's as clear as day they've given up pursuit,' Luther grumbled. 'So what are we still doing waiting around on the periphery of the Devil's Kitchen?'

'Well, it ain't safe to head back to the ranch, that's for sure,' Clarence argued. Things had not gone to plan. His idea had been to lure pursuers out into the Devil's Kitchen. All they'd find as they gave pursuit would be poisoned water holes. He'd chosen the place because he reckoned to know where the water holes were, having fled across the Kitchen many years back.

'Could be no one reckons we're worth bothering with,'

Luther stated bluntly.

Clarence shrugged. 'Well, I ain't convinced. There ain't no way Donald Ricket will dismiss us as being not worth bothering with. He's taken cash to see you dead, Luther Larkin, and is honour bound to fulfil the contract.'

'He ain't got any honour but he is sure as hell crazy,' Timberlee grumbled.

'And what of Marcus Cooper? I can't just forget about him, for he's done his damnedest to see me dead. Sooner or later there has to be a reckoning.'

'I've heard tell,' Clarence continued as if Luther had not spoken, 'that Ricket roasted a galoot he was real put out with, over a spit. And he'll be real put out with you, Luther Larkin, because he's made a bargain to see you dead and you did not oblige. He will not be kindly disposed towards you and that's a fact.'

'I don't give a damn!'

'So we may be in big trouble,' the oldster concluded. 'I'd guess folk are gonna be dying, but it won't be us. Anyone fool enough to try and hunt down Clarence Duffy will get his just deserts. And that goes for Donald Ricket. If he comes to Black Bear Crossing his luck is gonna run out and that's a fact.'

Luther stared out at the unrelenting sunlight blasting the salt pan, thinking that the salt crystals glinted like diamonds. There'd be bones on the pan, bones of men and horses who had tried to make it across; just staring out at the Kitchen made him feel that the moisture was being sucked from his skin. He wanted this over and done with. Hell, he'd had a bellyful of waiting; all those years waiting to get out of the state penitentiary and now having to wait in the wilderness, just in case pursuers were on their trail.

'Well, there ain't no help for it. I feel obliged to double back and check out the trail. You stay put and safeguard Miz Timberlee. Sooner or later our supplies will dwindle away.' Clarence shook his head. 'We'll think on what is best to do.'

'Well, the time for thinking is done,' snapped Luther. 'There's gonna be a showdown. I don't particularly want the old Grainger spread, but afer all the killing that's been done on account of that ranch I am damned if I'm gonna let Cooper take over the range.'

'Well, just you stay put till I've worked out what's best to be done,' replied Clarence.

'Hell, I sure hope he does not get himself killed,' Miz Timberlee declared. 'For I have become accustomed to the old coot.'

'He sure is put out that no one seems to want us dead enough to give pursuit,' Luther observed.

'Well, it's like a declaration we ain't worth a spit. Don't you be forgetting that Clarence Duffy was the Donald Ricket of his day.'

'I won't be forgetting because I never knew it. And them that did, well, I guess they're mostly dead.'

By the time he'd reached the small frontier town of Black Bear Crossing, Ricket had begun to realize that his men weren't with him on his quest for vengeance. They didn't give a damn that he'd been insulted. What drove them was the lure of wealth.

He'd been expecting resistance, so he played his final card. He told them that for all he cared they could take the town apart.

'Ride in and see what's going on!' he ordered, eyeing his man Fernandez. 'Let's see if anyone recognizes you!'

Fernandez spat. 'I doubt that they will.' Much to Ricket's surprise he unbuckled his two guns. 'I don't aim to call attention to myself.' He slumped in the saddle and pulled his hat down over his eyes, his whole demeanour changing. Then, kicking his horse's flanks, he rode towards Black Bear Crossing.

'Well, we must kick our heels until the varmint returns,' Ricket announced.

'Or not,' the man he called Salesman rejoined softly. 'If anyone needs to be dealt with before the boys hit town then I'm the man to do it.' He grinned unpleasantly. 'There ain't nothing I like better than catching folk by surprise, for I don't need recognition and glory. No insult to any of you intended.'

'None taken,' Ricket replied. When he had first met Salesman the man had introduced himself by saying that he preferred to think of himself as an old-time assassin rather than a fast gun.

Salesman, an underhand killer if ever there was one, simply grinned; short, fat and perspiring, the man looked nothing like the killer he was, a man who liked nothing better than to slit a throat or slide a blade between ribs. At one time the man had actually been a salesman before he had discovered his true calling, a revelation made easier by the fact that most folk underestimated his capabilities. Ricket never did, for, of all the men, Salesman was the most dangerous.

*

Kenna was in quandary. A man he had helped years back had turned up in his store, although at first he had not recognized the man as Fernandez.

'I owe you,' Fernandez had said, and had then delivered his warning before adding, 'Ricket has men watching the town so there ain't no way you can sneak out.' He had winked. 'I guess you know what to do,' Then he was gone.

Trouble was, Kenna did *not* know what to do now that Amos Standish was gone. Certainly he could not go to the replacement lawmen.

'You scrawny old buzzard. Harris is now the town's sheriff,' he had yelled. 'You come near my office with your petty complaints and I'll kick your butt so hard you'll end up in the next county.'

'The town is liable to turn on us,' he observed later to his wife. 'Folk have gone crazy around here. Why, look at the way the whole darn bunch of them joined up with Cooper and rode out to Luther's place, baying for blood. Why, they weren't no posse. All they were was a lynching party determined to hang three folk and one of them a woman. . . .' He paused. 'Leastways the three of them had sense to fork it out before Cooper and his vigilantes arrived.'

'Which is more than we can do before Ricket arrives.' Her voice shook.

'There ain't no one we can go to with this information without putting ourselves in danger. The only law in this town is the law of the gun!'

'I'm scared.'

So was he. 'We've got to be ready to squirrel ourselves away and wait until the trouble that's going to hit this town moves on. As it will! It's the only way.' He shrugged. 'If only Amos Standish had not decided to quit—'

'And left his wife destitute.'

'Now you know I cannot offer her credit.'

'Well, you won't be able to if Donald Ricket and his men take over the towm. They'll empty our shelves quick enough.' She gasped. 'He's one of them, I'm sure,' she hissed, staring out of the store, observing the newcomer riding into town.

He was a man so fat it was a wonder he did not buckle the legs of his unfortunate horse. Mercifully he headed on down Main Street towards the hotel.

Salesman bided his time, although it did not take him long to discover that, as regular as clockwork each Friday night Harris, the lawman put in place by Cooper, visited the saloon and 'partied' with one of the women. More important, Harris always left at the same time. Salesman always appreciated regularity, for it made his life easier when planning a kill.

A patient man, Salesman on the next Friday night simply concealed himself in an alleyway between the saloon and a neighbouring building. He waited patiently, not even counting the hours until the figure of the lawman lurched into sight. Indeed he could smell the stink of rot-gut whiskey even before he saw the man.

He'd killed in this way many times before. He didn't feel nervous nor did he hesitate, Moving silently for a rotund fellow he came up behind his victim and, grasping the man's long hair, pulled his head back and slit the drunken bum's throat before the man even realized he was under attack. The gurgling sounds as Harris drowned in his own blood didn't trouble Salesman none. He then dragged the corpse to the back of the alleyway and stowed it away behind the garbage. Lastly, he removed the long coat he was wearing and stowed it away in his salesman's bag.

Another job done without a hitch, he thought with satisfaction as he headed back to the hotel, knowing he'd dispatch the two so-called deputies with just as much ease. Folk might grin at the old stovepipe hat he wore, but it served a useful purpose.

At the hotel he went up to his room. He did not sleep but lay looking up at the ceiling. When his pocket watch told him it was breaking day and time to move he headed back down stairs and took a seat in the lobby.

The hotel clerk nodded at the salesman.

Salesman nodded back. He kept smiling. 'So tell me about this troublemaker Luther Larkin,' he encouraged, wanting to direct attention away from himself. He scarcely bothered to listen as the obliging clerk babbled away excitedly.

'I rode out to Larkin's spread myself.' The clerk smirked. 'But Larkin and that old-timer Clarence had already forked it out. We tracked them towards the Devil's Kitchen. But then decided to go no further, for they were as good as dead. We reckoned they died out on the salt flats. I sure was disappointed, for Rancher Cooper had vowed to bury the three of them up to their necks and leave them for the buzzards.'

'I prefer a good clean kill myself,' Salesman rejoined, watching the two burly sour-faced men coming down the stairs. 'Because I've always found . . .' He did not conclude his sentence.

'What the hell are you grinning at, fat man?' one of them challenged clearly intending to throw his weight around.

'Hell, Deputy, you'd be grinning if you knew what I know,' Salesman responded pleasantly.

'And what do you know?' the other snarled.

Salesman came to his feet. He was holding his old stovepipe hat.

'I'm gonna kick your butt,' the deputy started forward.

Salesman dropped the hat to reveal a levelled and ready Peacemaker. He fired almost immediately. He fired twice, hitting both men centre forehead. Then, unable to stop himself, he put a slug into the clerk's chest. 'It's best to finish the job.' He concluded his sentence.

A sound made him turn to confront a red-headed kid holding a pile of clean laundry, which he was obviously delivering. Salesman would have shot him as well except for the fact that the kid suddenly grinned.

'Great shooting, mister,' he congratulated. 'Hey, do you still need your stovepipe?'

'Well, I can see you have the makings of a mighty fine killer.'

'Gee! Thanks, mister.' Then, clearly not wanting to test his good luck further, the kid bolted.

Salesman chuckled. Clearly the kid had thought he was about to be blasted. Leastways he'd known when to bolt.

Tommy Kelly raced home to get his ma. He was no fool. He knew bad things were about to happen in Black Bear Crossing. Two deputies and the hotel clerk had been killed and the fat man had just sat there, grinning. Tommy didn't need to be smart to know that Ricket would be riding in soon.

The only place he could think of to take his ma was the livery barn, where that crazy old coot who had a soft spot for his ma might hide her in his hayloft.

'Get up there.' The oldster waved his pitchfork at Mrs Kelly, who'd been dragged into the barn by her boy. 'Whilst you have a chance,' he encouraged.

'Get up there, Ma,' Tommy yelled. 'Unless you want to see me shot down trying to protect you.'

At that his ma, much to his relief, scrambled up into the hayloft. And the ostler quickly whipped away the ladder for he knew the kid had no intention of hiding.

'Tommy!'

'Don't fret, Ma. I'll crawl beneath the sidewalk,' With that Tommy was gone.

'Now don't you fret, Mrs Kelly, young ones are generally safe unless they're gunned down in error, for there is no glory to be had in blasting them. Now hush up, ma'am, for they are riding in. Lord help us all,' he added. No doubt they'd soon be in his barn telling him to take care of the horses. 'For the Lord's sake don't make a sound, Mrs Kelly. I reckon I am safe for they'll want the horses tended. Lord help this town, for the only law now is the law of the gun.'

Tommy had squirrelled himself away beneath the sidewalk. Now he watched in amazement as Mrs Standish, yelling and screaming, was hefted over a man's shoulder and carried away. And the rest of the churchgoing women were faring in similar fashion. Most of them were being dragged, kicking and screeching, towards the saloon. Even

Reverend Dent's wife and Mrs Robins were grabbed. Tommy was suddenly glad he'd seen to his ma's safety.

'I'm gonna see to it those varmints eat dirt.' The ostler heard the words before the large man dressed in black save for a silver waistcoat came into the barn.

'You've sold my man's horse on, ain't you ostler?' Ricket challenged.

'No sir – Mr Ricket. I've kept the critter here ready for when you came to town,' the ostler replied, indicating the animal.

'Well, it seems your good sense has saved your hide. Tend to the horses.'

'Yes sir – Mr Ricket.'

Paying no further attention to the ostler, Ricket strode out on to Main Street. He headed for the saloon. He'd make the place his base for his short sojourn in Black Bear Crossing: short, but unforgettable for some, that was for sure.

CHAPTER 9

From his hiding place Tommy Kelly watched as terror took hold of the town. He could not believe that the men whom he had been obliged to heed proved useless when it came to protecting themselves. They all lacked the backbone to put up any kind of fight.

Women were fighting, he saw, but their kicking and screaming didn't help them none. There were no Miz Timberlees among these women.

Hell-fire preacher the Reverend Dent, Tommy observed, was strangely silent. He knew better than to threaten any of these men with hell fire even though his wife had been dragged into the saloon. Tommy, hearing the women screaming, was mighty glad his ma was not among them. Nor was Mrs Kenna, he realized. There was no sign of Kenna either although the renegades were looting the store and helping themselves to whatever caught their fancy.

Maybe when things had quietened down he could sneak in and help himself. He watched as the men were herded together on Main Street, all of them keeping their eyes lowered, each fearful that he would be the one singled out for attention. That crazy old man Clarence would not have been so amenable, Tommy thought, nor would Luther Larkin.

'So none of you good folk considered my man worth burying decent.' Ricket shook his head. 'So what I'm gonna do is have you men folk taken to the cemetery and put to work digging a grave. You don't need shovels. Your bare hands will suffice. It don't matter Ollie's bones ain't being laid to rest, for I've always believed it is the thought that counts.' He paused. 'And whilst you are digging you can ask yourself who best deserves to occupy that grave, apart from Rancher Cooper, that is.'

Fernandez was pleased to see that the Kennas were not amongst the folk rounded up. They'd done him a good turn once, for they had taken him in when he'd been dumped more dead than alive out on Main Street. He owed them. They had heeded his warning and were lying low until this was over. This reminded him that he was a man who believed in settling his debts. And collecting his dues! The Coppers certainly owed him. He had found a fitting way to deal with Marcus Cooper. But the one he hated real bad was Maybelle Copper.

He knew darn well where the storekeepers were hiding out, but he reckoned no one else did. Just as well! The inhabitants of this two-bit town would not think twice about ratting on one of their own if they thought it would ease their predicament.

'Well, what do you know?' The ostler kept up a commentary, though talking to himself. 'I reckon the men are headed for the cemetery whilst the womenfolk have been dragged into the saloon. Well, I reckon a man can draw his own conclusions. Thank the Lord for quick-thinking boys, I say.'

Mrs Kelly, up in his hayloft, kept silent. He'd had to cuss her plenty before she had agreed not to say a word. The ostler did not trust folk in this town not to give away their own. Not that any of the unfortunate womenfolk in the saloon would be thinking of her whereabouts. Gun law had taken over the town and now it was everyone for themselves. She prayed silently for the torment of the town to end quickly without death.

Ricket made himself comfortable in the saloon. He'd taken precautions. No one was going to be able to sneak out of town, that was for sure. Anyone trying to ride in or out was to be blasted from the saddle. Without exception!

'Get me a horse saddled pronto.' The town's blacksmith entered the livery barn. 'I'm gonna alert Marcus Cooper. He'll deal with those killers without working up a sweat.'

'Now you're talking nonsense. You don't stand a chance in hell!' the ostler advised. 'Do you think he ain't thought about folk trying to sneak out of town! Best thing—'

'Quit gabbing and get me a horse. There ain't no telling what that varmint is going to do. Someone has got to save this town. We need the ranchers and their men here pronto!'

'You will be gunned down, you damn fool!' The ostler did not sound particularly concerned. 'There ain't no need to risk yourself. They've let me be as I am an ostler, and they'll let you be as you are a blacksmith. Men know that out here they depend on their horses. Without a good horse under him many a man has come to a bad end, for this land is harsh and unyielding.'

'Get my horse, damn you, or I'll break your scrawny neck!'

Mrs Kelly heard muffled curses and then the sound of a horse leaving the barn. A shot immediately followed.

'Damn fool ain't even got a head left now,' the ostler observed. 'And it ain't as if I did not warn him. Ricket has put a man to watch the livery barn.'

Lying flat in the dirt, head craned upward in a way which would give him a neck crick, Tommy Kelly watched as a dishevelled Mrs Standish burst out of the saloon followed by Mrs Dent, equally dishevelled. Both women were screaming. Tommy's mouth dropped open as he watched men dragging both women back inside.

'If you don't need me, boss, I'll take a walk down to the cemetery. I want to see how the digging is progressing.' Fernandez had shown no interest in any of the townswomen.

Ricket grinned. 'You want to see those varmints sweat!'

Fernandez nodded. 'Damn right I do. Damn right.'

His features hidden by a wild untamed beard he was unrecognizable as the young ranch hand who had once worked for Marcus Cooper. He'd done nothing wrong. Maybelle Cooper had smiled at him and he had smiled back; no reason for her to tell her husband he'd been making unwelcome advances. He'd been beaten to an unrecognizable lump of meat at the Cooper ranch and then dumped on Main Street.

He'd realized later that she done what she did deliberately, to get him a beating. Well, sometime soon he aimed to meet up again with Maybelle. It was time to split from Ricket, for the man was becoming more and more delusional. He'd taken the town apart without thought of the consequences. Now every decent man's hand would be against them for what they'd done to the women of Black Bear Crossing.

'And that's what happens to any man who disrespects Mrs Cooper,' the rancher had warned the town. He'd gotten away with it. He'd never been held to account. Why, if it had not been for Kenna haranguing a reluctant lawman they would have left him without medical care.

'There's something about Mrs Cooper that I do not much care for,' the storekeeper had said by way of explanation for having taken Fernandez in.

Well, Kenna had never said a truer word!

Fernandez sauntered down to the cemetery. He ignored the glimpse he caught of a kid hiding beneath the sidewalk.

As he passed the store he saw that it was being looted. That was to be expected. He reckoned they would not find Kenna. No one had noticed that the exterior of the store looked slightly larger than the interior, Kenna having constructed a false wall behind the shelves, a kind of hideaway for times such as these.

He grinned when he saw the men of the town down on their knees scraping at the dirt with their bare hands, egged on by the threat that anyone who stopped digging would have his hand blasted off. Fernandez recognized the preacher and the lawyer. Even as he watched the lawyer collapsed, clutching at his chest.

'Leave him be,' a hardcase growled. Threats and curses

did indeed encourage Robins's fellow townsmen to leave him be.

'Hell, it's gonna be a long day and a long night,' a man observed with a guffaw. He scratched his head. 'Hell, I reckon he ain't joshing!' He pointed at Robins. 'Heart just done let him down. Leastways his misery is over.' He guffawed again. They all did.

Shouting woke Tommy Kelly from an uneasy sleep. He was so stiff he felt as though he could scarcely move. He moved his arms and legs as best he could just in case he was obliged to make a run for safety. He'd sneaked out sometime during the night and had helped himself to the gun carried by the dead blacksmith who had now become a magnet for files as he had been left where he lay on Main Street. Tommy had also sneaked into Kenna's silent store and helped himself to sweets and some kind of fancy sausage that his ma could not afford to buy.

He'd forked it out pronto when he'd heard snuffling sounds coming from a wall. Only later did he work out that it was only the Kennas hiding out.

Unknown to his ma, Tommy knew how to fire a gun. Good enough, he reckoned, to earn himself a place with Ricket. Only fear of his ma leaving her hiding-place had kept him from marching into the saloon, bold as you please, to announce he wanted to hire out.

Ricket had put one of the terrified women to brewing coffee and frying bacon and eggs, courtesy of the town store. He ate quickly, keen to be gone, recognizing that there was only a short time during which a town could be safely taken over and brought to its knees.

117

'I ain't never seen such a bunch of yellow-bellies as I have seen in this town,' the gunman taunted the shame-faced men. 'The knowledge of what you are will stay with you as long as your miserable lives last.' He raised his voice. 'Well, you all know that I'm here on account of Marcus Cooper. Now what I need to find out is whether he is as yellow as the rest of you. Only time will tell! He paused. 'Now I'm gonna pass a hat around and each one of you men is to write down the name of the man you reckon ought to hang for dumping Ollie out in the scrub. Anyone will do except Cooper, for hanging is too good for that no-account.'

Outside on Main Street men were plunging their heads into the horse trough, whilst a few others were heaving up the contents of their stomachs, for liquor had flowed last night. But Ricket knew they'd all be ready to ride, for he had promised to blast anyone who wasn't fit to sit the saddle.

When he had finished the remains of his breakfast he announced the results of the citizens' ballot. With the exception of one person they had all voted for the under-taker.

Tommy watched as a rope with a noose at one end was thrown over a branch of the ancient tree out on Main Street. He gulped as he realized what Ricket aimed to do.

'No surprises there.' Ricket made a great show of count-ing the votes. 'One of you has voted for Reverend Dent, I see. But the overall winner can only be the undertaker. String him up!' Tommy watched as the terrified under-taker, begging for his life, was placed astride a horse.

'Well, undertaker, there ain't one person in this two-bit

118

town man enough to save you. I want you to know that just as I want the so-called men of this town to know what they really are. They might walk on two legs but sure as hell they ain't men!'

Ricket whooped and whacked the horse carrying the undertaker. Then, to Tommy's surprise they all rode out, leaving Crisp kicking frantically.

The townsmen stood as if rooted, all of them too damn scared to save one of their own.

'He's damn right! You're all of you yellow-bellies,' Tommy hollered as he emerging from under the sidewalk. In his hand he held the blacksmith's shooter. Sighting the weapon he took a pot shot at the rope, missed, then tried again. The rope severed and the undertaker fell gasping to the ground. But Tommy didn't care about Crisp. All he'd wanted was to show his shooting skills. No one stepped forward to tell him to mind his manners. More to the point there was no sign of Ricket returning. 'I'm the only man in town,' he announced proudly. No one dared contradict him.

He pointed at Crisp who lay gurgling on the floor. 'Well, ain't one of you gonna move his necktie?'

His moment was spoiled however by his ma, who came rushing down Main Street. Seeing the expression on her face, he took off in the opposite direction.

'Go fetch Marcus Cooper. Go fetch Marcus Cooper,' Mrs Dent screamed. 'They deserve to die.' She rounded on her husband. 'An eye for an eye,' she screamed.

Marcus Cooper realized that he had been cornered. He was now part of whatever devious game Ricket was playing.

119

Personally, he did not give a damn about the town and its cowardly inhabitants. But the day was coming when he'd need their votes. He would not get them until harsh punishment had been dealt out.

The neighbouring ranchers, genuinely outraged by the killer, had banded together and he, as the largest ranch owner, was expected to lead them.

He found himself hoping that Ricket would be fool enough to head into the Devil's Kitchen, as had Luther Larkin. Very few pursuers would care to risk their hides by venturing out on to the salt flats. But he doubted whether the gunman would prove so accommodating. Larkin had been desperate to avoid capture. Ricket clearly would be planning to spring an ambush.

'Well, it's as plain as day that Ricket is a twisted galoot, a mad dog that must be put down and that's what we're gonna do. We're gonna hang every last one of them high!'

Well, the three hardcases he'd hired at considerable expense had proved themselves useless. It would not have been so easy to get the jump on Standish. Nor would Standish have allowed himself to be gunned down by a fat clown wearing a stovepipe hat under which a Peacemaker had been concealed. A so-called salesman of ladies' corsetry, the man had claimed to be, and the fools in town had taken the man at face value.

'We must keep our eyes peeled and our wits about us. That varmint intends to spring an ambush, for he ain't man enough to face us!'

He'd send men to scout ahead, watching out for likely places that that crazy son of a bitch might select for ambush.

'Well, the Scotsman is not coming,' one of the assembled ranchers declared. 'His boys wanted to ride along but the old man forbade it, said he was not fighting your battles for you and that you'd brought this mess down on the town.'

'Well, the Scotsman is talking out of the back of his hat.' Truth was he had his eyes on the Scotsman's ranch. 'Well, it's to be expected; the man is new to the territory.'

'Just as well,' one of Cooper's men announced loudly. 'The Scotsman and his boys would slow us down plenty. We all know it! They are nothing but greenhorns.'

Maybelle, standing on the porch watching the assembled men, felt decidedly uneasy. She could see, even if her husband could not, that events were spiralling out of control. Of course if anything happened to Marcus she'd have the ranch. She'd sell up and get out of the territory, she decided. Things had started going wrong ever since Luther Larkin had come back to town.

To this day she could not understand why Walt had made his ridiculous deathbed confession. True, she hadn't had much to do with him. Their paths had seldom crossed once she had wed Marcus. She suspected he had guessed she had put Higgy Shaw up to convincing Amos Standish that Luther Larkin had made threats against Hamish Cooper.

Well, Higgy was dead and it could only have been Miz Timberlee who'd killed him. Too bad she'd chosen Luther's buggy to hide out in. Anyone else would have given her up, but not Luther Larkin.

Marcus Cooper nodded curtly to his wife. She was to blame for this mess. She'd been the one to insist they get in a hired gun, namely Donald Ricket. Hell, he should never have listened to her!

'Let's ride.' He could not bring himself to look at Maybelle as he knew deep down that if he were killed she'd move on soon enough. Maybe it was time to think of ridding himself of her. Like everyone else, she was not indispensable.

'Well, leastways the varmint did not try to burn the town, unlike that bum Luther Larkin,' he observed as he led the men into town. He could not help but notice that Kenna and his wife, standing before their store, looked in a decidedly better state than the rest of the folk.

'It's about time you got here. All this is your doing.' To Cooper's disbelief Kenna was actually laying the blame on his shoulders. 'You know you should have let Larkin be. You've brought grief to this town and that's a fact.'

Cooper ignored the storekeeper. That was all he could do for now.

But no one else, Cooper quickly realized, would meet his eye. An air of shame hung over the town.

There were bodies on the sidewalk. His three men, and another one whom he knew to be the blacksmith although, with his head blasted, the man was unrecognizable, and Robins. He did his best to feign concern.

A dishevelled woman burst from the hotel. She ran screaming down Main Street, eyes wide and vacant.

'You!' she pointed at him. 'You brought this pestilence to our town,' she screamed.

Reverend Dent emerging from the hotel, grabbed his wife's arm and hauled her back towards the hotel. To Cooper's astonishment Mrs Dent turned on her husband, scratching wildly at his face.

'We're looking to you, Rancher Cooper,' a man said. 'It's only right. That renegade came here on account of you. Why he did not ride out directly to your spread I cannot say. I wish the hell he had, for this town has suffered. Men have died. Decent women cannot hold their heads up high. This town has been shamed.' He paused. 'I'm telling you now that unless you make things right there's no place for you in this town. And there ain't nothing you can do to make things right except hunt that mad dog down and hang him high.'

CHAPTER 10

Marcus Cooper realized that his standing and authority in town was gone. There was only one way he could get it back. He had no choice. He had to run down that mad dog Donald Ricket.

He went on the attack. 'So not one of you was man enough to do anything when the womenfolk were being abused.' He nodded. 'Just as I thought, and now you are looking to better men, ranching men, to bring those varmints to judgment.'

'Not one of us would have stood a chance against those gunmen! And you know it,' a man countered, answering back in a way he would have never have dared do before Ricket's descent upon the town.

'And your men were no damn use! Well you can bet your life Amos Standish would have done a damn sight better. Seems odd don't it, he was laid low with some kind of poison just before Oliver Lewis came to town?'

'Now that ain't right,' a ranching man spoke up. 'That crazy old woman poisoned Slim. And then she poisoned Amos because she knew she would have been arrested for murder.'

'Well, it seems to me someone paid her to poison Amos. But he got short measure when it came to lacing the food because Slim was the one she wanted to do away with. As I recall I saw Dolly and Miz Maybelle sharing a pot of tea. Real cosy they looked!'

'Why, you no-account varmint . . .' Cooper grabbed the man by his shirt front.

'What are you gonna do, Mr Cooper? Shoot everyone in the town who speaks out of turn? You're gonna have to gun down the whole town because we are all of the same mind concerning what's been going on in Black Bear Crossing. You took us for fools but we ain't!'

With a shove Cooper sent the speaker sprawling on the sidewalk. He fought to control the red-hot rage that swept through him. Right now he'd like nothing better than to kick the hell out of the galoot who'd dared to accuse Maybelle. Folk in town should know to keep their lips buttoned when it came to the Coopers.

'I'm going to make allowances for the accusations that have been hurled my way.' He took a deep breath. 'I'm mindful that no one in this town is in their right mind after what Ricket has done. I promise you all that I'm going to see that Donald Ricket and his band of killers are run down and given their just deserts. And if any of you think a rope is too good for those no-account killers I'll think of ways to dispatch them in a fitting manner.'

'We're counting on you, Mr Cooper.' The ostler pushed his way through the crowd. 'Ain't that right, men?'

'What makes you think you can handle Donald Ricket. You couldn't even handle Luther Larkin.' Mrs Robins was the speaker. 'No, you had to hire a killer and now my husband is dead because of what you've done. He was forced to dig until his nails were broken and bleeding, until he could take no more.'

'I don't want to hear Larkin's name mentioned again,' said Cooper. 'It's him who has brought grief on the town. We won't be seeing him again for he is either bleached bones somewhere out in the Devil's Kitchen or fleeing for his life. And as he won't be back I'm claiming Walt's old spread. That's only right, for it should have passed to Maybelle on her brother's death.'

An uncomfortable silence greeted his words.

'If you're aiming to claim exclusive right to the Big Muddy you'll have a range war on your hands,' warned Mrs Robins.

'Nothing will change,' Cooper lied. 'You have my word on that. Now I'll not ask any of you folk from town to ride along with us. You can leave it to us ranching men to take care of Ricket. Once he is dead you folk will feel a mite better.'

'Well, all I have got to say to you, Marcus Cooper, is don't show your face in our town again until Ricket is dead.' Mrs Robins was determined to have the last word. 'And furthermore this town will find its own lawman, a man of the calibre of Sheriff Amos Standish.'

To hell with Amos Standish and the rest of them, Cooper thought. The townsfolk had indeed turned against him. There would be no turning back this time. He had to run down Donald Ricket. The man had to pay for what he had done to this town. Cooper never would have imagined that the day would come when he would be openly disrespected by women. He knew that until Ricket

126

paid for his crimes there was not a damn thing he could do to regain his standing.

Luther sat by the campfire, the journal Crisp had given him open on his knees. As they waited on the periphery of the Devil's Kitchen he had been passing his time deciphering Walt's journal. It had been damn hard working out the code in which Walt had chosen to write. But, clear as day, Walt had had little choice but to use a code, for he would not have wanted just anyone to read what he had written.

Walt Grainger had every reason to feel guilty. Luther saw now that rather than tarnish his good name Walt had kept silent about what he'd seen the day Hamish Cooper had been murdered. It had been damn hot: hotter than anyone could remember, so folk had said. More than one person had sneaked out to the Big Muddy, the only watering hole that had not run dry.

Walt had made it a habit of long standing to conceal himself up on the bluff overlooking the Big Muddy. From there he would spy on folk taking a dip. He had seen the real killer but had chosen not to say so.

A woman had killed Hamish but it had not been Maybelle. Well, who would have believed it, Luther thought? She'd gotten away with it. No one would ever have suspected her or even been much aware of her existence.

He decided he was going to keep what he had learned to himself. He didn't give a damn about any of it now. He had no interest in denouncing another, especially as it seemed Hamish had brought grief upon himself. Tempers had been frayed during that particular hot spell, he recalled.

'Just why are you staring at me, Luther Larkin?' Miz Timberlee snapped, misinterpreting his expression as one of interest in herself. 'Well, spit it out.' She was clearly in a bad mood.

'I can't say, Miz Timberlee,' he blurted out.

She nodded. 'Well, I think I can guess what's on your mind!'

'And the fact is I'd be obliged if you—'

He'd been about to say he'd be obliged if she didn't ask what he'd discovered from the journal. But Miz Timberlee, he soon realized, didn't give a damn about Walt's journal.

'Say no more, Luther Larkin,' she declared rising to her feet. She smiled. 'Come on over here and I'll be happy to show you all you need to know about womenfolk.'

'Miz Timberlee . . .' he croaked, 'I. . . .'

'No need to thank me, Luther. I understand. You're in dire need. 'With that she beckoned to him.

He took a deep breath. He didn't know much about womenfolk but Clarence was always yapping how Miz Timberlee in some ways reminded him of his late wife. And Clarence's late wife, from what Luther had gathered, would have thought nothing of killing a man who had disrespected her. Moreover, he didn't want to risk offending Miz Timberlee. Her sharp-shooting had saved his life.

Come to think of it, Higgy Shaw had met an untimely end at her hands. She wasn't a woman he wanted to rile. It could be risky. He stood up, took a deep breath and tossed

Walt's journal upon the fire before heading towards her.

Hell, if he had to choose between Miz Timberlee and Maybelle Cooper, why he was a damn sight better off choosing Miz Timberlee because Maybelle – why she was best described as a snake in the grass, and that was speaking kindly.

If anyone had dared to ask him, Donald Ricket would never have been able to explain what drove him to do what he did. When he'd been terrorizing the town he had never felt better. He enjoyed seeing the fear his presence occasioned in lesser folk. He liked to hear women scream and see men tremble in their boots.

He was planning to make an example of Marcus Cooper which would have folk talking for years to come. That others would die alongside the rancher did not trouble him in the slightest. If they were fool enough to believe they could best him, hunt him down like a dog, then they deserved what came their way.

As for Luther Larkin, word was the man had perished in a place called the Devil's Kitchen. He'd think about that later.

It had actually been Fernandez who had come up with the plan for dealing with Marcus Cooper. Fernandez hated Marcus Cooper with a vengeance. 'He'll be expecting to be bushwhacked,' Fernandez had said, adding that bullets were too good for Cooper.

Ricket had agreed.

'They'll die a terrible death but I do not need to witness it. Let me be the one to wait concealed. Let me be the one to spring the trap,' Fernandez had begged.

'Well if your trap fails I'll have your hide. I ain't joshing.'

'I won't fail. I've waited years for this time to come.'

'Well I guess you have. I'll not deny you, then.'

Now Ricket waited for the fools to ride unwittingly into the trap. There sure was an unpleasant surprise awaiting them at the end of this particular trail.

'Ricket ain't even attempting to hide his trail,' Dave Collins, a fellow rancher whose spread in no way equalled the Cooper ranch, stated the obvious. 'I smell a rat. We're being led into a trap.'

Marcus Cooper sighed impatiently. 'Unless I am mistaken the man is headed straight towards Box canyon. Once we're through the Box there are wooded hills overlooking the trail, perfect places for ambush, I'd say. That's when he'll make his move, once we're through Box Canyon.'

There were murmurs of agreement.

'We'll leave the trail. We'll flush him out of the woods.' Cooper could see that the initial enthusiasm for hunting Ricket down was beginning to evaporate. 'We'll see to it that the varmint tastes hell!' The rancher raised his fist sky high. 'Ain't that so? He'll pay for what he did to our town, to our women.'

'You'd best face the fact that we may not be able to run him to ground,' Collins grumbled.

'He'll stop running and set up an ambush.' Cooper shook his head. 'That's why the varmint terrorized the town. What he did was a means to an end, that end being for us to ride into his trap. He knew darn well he'd lose

130

men if he set about my ranch head on. So he damn well fixed things so that I'd have to go after him.'

'Well, the man's plan seems to be working so far.'

'Hell, forgive me for thinking I have townsfolk riding with me. Anyone who wants to quit can do so.'

To his surprise a handful of men, shamefaced it was true, elected to ride back towards the town.'

'Keep on riding, you damn yellow-bellies. I don't want to see any of you hereabouts again or I might be tempted to blast you as you deserve,' he yelled at the backs of the turncoats, wishing he could pull his rifle and shoot a few of them down as they deserved. 'Let's ride!'

The remaining men picked up Ricket's trail and found that the man was indeed headed into Box Canyon.

The canyon was a narrow belt of land winding its way between towering hills, sheer rock rose on either side, with scrub sprouting from the parched soil. Every now and then a stray steer blundered from the scrub, lowered its horns, then crashed back out of sight.

Concealed, Fernandez watched the man he hated above all others rein in his men at the entrance to Box Canyon. He was afraid for a moment that the rancher would not follow the tracks left by Ricket and the others into the canyon. But all Cooper was doing was allowing them a moment of rest, for the day was hotter than hell.

Fernandez had never forgotten how Marcus Cooper had beaten him to within an inch of his life, all because Miz Maybelle had falsely accused him of making advances. After Cooper had finished Fernandez had borne no resemblance to the good-looking youth he had been. He hadn't forgotten about Miz Maybelle either. He had a surprise in store for her once her husband had been taken care of. She'd watched him being beaten and had not said a word to try and stop her crazed husband.

It was too bad, he thought, that Marcus Cooper would never know just who had brought about his downfall. But then no doubt Marcus Cooper wouldn't even remember the name of the young cowpoke he'd near killed all those years back.

On the high rim overlooking Box Canyon Ricket waited for Cooper's hunting party to appear. Salesman sat apart from the rest of the men. He busied himself by whittling away at a piece of wood.

'We're going in. Keep your eyes peeled.' Cooper moved forward, knowing the rest of them had no choice but to follow or be labelled cowards. 'There's dead meat, I'd say.' He pointed at the small circling specks visible against the cloudless sky. He smiled mirthlessly. 'It's too much to hope the varmints have had a falling out!'

Fernandez heaved a sigh of relief as the hunting party moving slowly headed into the canyon. By the time Cooper realized that he had ridden into a trap it would be too damn late to get out.

It had taken Fernandez quite a while to realize that Maybelle Cooper had been deliberately setting him up for a beating. Deliberately she'd smiled at him and fluttered her eyelashes, knowing he'd smile back. Slowly he had become to realize what she was. A former beau, Hamish Cooper, had been found dead by the creek and the son of the town drunk had been convicted of the crime. Well, he guessed she'd had a hand in that as well.

He took out his matches. He moved towards the mouth of the canyon, a tin of kerosene in his hand. The time had come to split from Ricket. He was going after Maybelle Cooper. It was payback time. He'd waited for years and now fate had dealt the cards which he had needed to settle old scores.

He dropped to his knees, set fire to kindling and shielded the flame with his hands. A slight breeze was blowing which would carry the flames into the canyon. The dry scrub would go up like tinder. Cooper and his men would ride as though the devil were on their tail. But it would do them no good, for the narrow entrance leading from the canyon would have been blocked, courtesy of Donald Ricket.

CHAPTER 11

Halfway into the canyon Marcus Cooper called a halt. He uncorked his canteen and allowed a mouthful of tepid water to trickle down his parched throat. It was damn hot. Sweat trickled between his shoulder blades, dampening his shirt. Angrily he swatted a fly which had just bitten him beneath his left eye. From experience he knew the eye would swell as the bite filled with pus and partly obscured his vision.

'Pesky flies,' he muttered to no one in particular. Small dots continued to circle in the clear blue sky; harbingers of death, he thought.

'Maybe one less for us to deal with,' Dave Collins observed laconically.

'Or maybe the varmint has set a trap to draw us in,' a townsman who had ridden along to see justice done observed uncertainly.

'Box Canyon ain't exactly a spot I'd choose for a shoot-out.' Marcus Cooper contemptuously dismissed the man's concern. He gestured at the spiked shrubs. 'Anyone fool enough to put foot amongst those goddamn bushes would soon find themselves ripped to ribbons.'

'Well, you are right about that,' Dave Collins agreed.

'Now, any of you men who are running scared had best make sure you don't blast one of our own,' Cooper warned. 'The only critters we will find coming out of those bushes are rogue steers of the four-legged variety.'

Someone laughed and the tension they were all feeling eased.

Dave Collins didn't laugh. Hell, he thought, Cooper ought to have taken care of his own grievances with Luther Larkin without bringing in a hired gunman.

'Well, I guess we must get on with the job we came here to do. The town is looking to us ranching men for justice,' Cooper announced as he urged his horse forward once more. He did not look back to see if the others followed. He was pretty sure that none of them could back out without losing face.

He rode slowly. And he kept his eyes peeled, although there was no fallen rock formation in this canyon from behind which an ambush could be sprung. Although the day was sweltering the breeze blowing through the £anyon provided a welcome relief. He began to relax, for all was quiet enough. His ears heard no sounds made by hidden-away horses, no answering whinnies from the sounds made by their own horses. He could hear nothing but the buzzing of flies and the occasional chirp of a bird.

'Hell, I wish I was anywhere else but here,' a waddy griped. 'Hell, I wish I was back at Slim's forking down one of old Dolly's meat pies.'

'Hush up now!' Marcus Cooper raised a hand, aware

that he had yellow-bellies among the men; just the thought of taking on Ricket was making them sweat plenty.

'You damn fool,' a man hissed. 'That old critter done for Slim and near killed Sheriff Standish.'

'Hush up, I say,' repeated Marcus. 'Now's not the time to be talking of an old woman with addled wits. We have more important matters to think on than a crazy old critter.' He guessed her wits were not that addled for she'd forked it before he could get around to making sure she never told what she had been paid to do. And why the hell had she killed the man who had given her a job and let that damn thorn in his side, Amos Standish, keep on breathing?

Dolly watched as the scenery sped past. She was headed east, determined to turn her back upon the frontier. She was different now; her clothes were smart and new, thanks to Maybelle's cash.

Her gloved hands tightly clutched a carpetbag crammed full of bills, for Slim, her late employer, had never trusted banks. She'd known all along where he hid his cash but had never dared take even one bill. Not that she'd poisoned him to steal his cash; no, his oafish manner towards her had been his downfall. After all, she'd ensured that Amos Standish had merely been laid low. Her conscience was clear.

The other matter did not trouble her either, although she had at first lived in fear of being denounced. But no one had paid her any mind. She was just old Dolly, the skivvy from Slim's restaurant, a woman denied respect by any of them. The fact was, it would be a while before any of the varmints in town got around to even noticing she was gone. No one ever thought about her and that was good.

She'd never thought that she would be the one to kill Hamish Cooper. Indeed, it was entirely his own fault, foul-mouthed young varmint that he had been,

It had been hotter than hell that summer, she recalled, and she'd sneaked out of town wanting a dip in Big Muddy Creek. Hamish had showed up and he'd been pretty mad at seeing her. He'd yelled all manner of abuse and told her to get out of his sight. She guessed he'd been waiting for Maybelle Grainger, as she was then.

She hadn't snapped until he'd picked up a sharpish stone and hurled it her way with a volley of insults. It had struck her head, made her bleed; she still had a small white scar as a reminder of that day.

So she hurled a rock herself, jagged and sharp, which had left him staggering and confused, giving her time to grab up something a darn sight bigger with which to set about young Hamish. And set about him she did. Afterwards she cleaned up and got herself back into town without being seen, never thinking that that damn fool Luther Larkin would find the body and raise the alarm.

He'd looked at her from his jail cell when she had shuffled in with the victuals. But he'd never said a word. Yep, like the rest he'd looked and never really seen. But maybe Walt Grainger had seen something that day, for he'd always eyed her mighty peculiar when he saw her around town. She guessed he must have done. But if he had seen her why the hell had he not spoken up? Suddenly she understood. Walt could not have spoken up without losing his good name. She saw what he'd been doing: hiding somewhere overlooking the water and watching folk taking a dip in states of undress.

She smiled grimly, recalling how she'd pounded away at Hamish's head until her arms had ached and her breath was ragged. Walt would have watched that. Well, she guessed she had hit upon the truth. Walt's good name had meant a good deal more than seeing justice done. He'd watched an innocent boy railroaded rather than risk losing his good name.

Setting back against the upholstery she watched as the landscape rushed past. This time round fate had dealt her a good hand, but it had sure dealt Marcus Cooper a dud when Luther Larkin returned to town.

'What the hell!' Marcus Cooper could not credit the sight which met his eyes. 'Hell, I always knew Ricket was a sick son of a bitch and this proves it.'

Clearly Ricket had made camp, as evidenced by the remains of a dead campfire and a discarded coffee pot. He'd been pretty damn careful as well, choosing bare rock floor upon which to set his fire. Scrub round about had been cleared, for the Box Canyon at this time of year was tinder dry. He'd caught a stray steer, butchered the animal and cooked a meal, as evidenced by a discarded, blackened fry pan.

The unused remains of the butchered steer lay some distance away from where the campfire had been. Buzzards flapped away at the men's approach and were immediately replaced by a heaving mass of flies which more or less ignored the riders. But the remains of the butchered critter were not the focal point of their stares.

Their focal point was a large boulder, and upon that boulder Ricket had set up the head of the critter, even placing a high Stetson upon the critter's head. Its eyes had been picked out, Cooper noted. Insults pertaining to him had been charcoaled upon the rock.

'Crazy son of a bitch.' Dave Collins, uttering a snort of disgust, spurred his horse forward and kicked the offending sight from the boulder. 'Hanging is too good for that polecat and so is a goddamn slug!' He voiced the thoughts of them all.

Cooper, whose mouth had been gaping open, snapped it shut. 'I'm gonna skin that varmint,' he vowed. 'You hear me now! I want him taken alive. I don't give a damn about the rest of them but Ricket I want alive!'

From the high rim of the canyon the man they were talking about watched with glee the reactions of the men discovering his little surprise. He made no effort to conceal himself, knowing that one of the dumb varmints was bound to spot him.

'Hell boss, there he is!' One of Cooper's crew pointed upwards at the distant rim of the canyon.

Even though he guessed the gesture would be futile Cooper took up his rifle, aimed, and fired skywards, knowing that the distance was too great for his slug to do damage.

'Could be the varmints are doubling back. How many men have you left guarding your spread, Mr Cooper?' The townsman sounded real worried.

'Not damn near enough!' Dave Collins exclaimed.

'Ricket could hit any one of us. Our unguarded spreads

are sitting targets for that no account varmint,' continued the anxious townsman.

'It's my place he'll go for.' Cooper squinted upwards, surprised to see the watcher; presumably the gunman himself had not withdrawn. 'Hell! I've got my wife to think of, my Maybelle.'

'He won't have that much of a head start if he can't use the box to double back. He'll be obliged to take the long route. We can beat him back.'

'Most of us have womenfolk to think of.' Collins was practically shouting. 'And the fact is, Mr Cooper, we must protect our own. We have no choice. So, much I as I would like to go on. . . .' He shrugged.

Cooper nodded. 'Cowardly varmint is counting on us turning back on account of we can't *know* what is in his mind but hitting our womenfolk *seems* to be what he has in mind. And I ain't arguing about turning back. As I've said, we've all got womenfolk to think of.'

'What the hell is that smell?' a waddy exclaimed. 'And I ain't talking about rotted meat.'

Dave Collins was the first to notice the curling black smoke marring the perfect blue of the sky.

'Hell, Marcus, you have led us into a trap!' he accused. 'That devil has had one of his men set fire to the scrub. He aims to burn us alive.'

'Let's get the hell out of here,' Cooper, suddenly in fear for his life, raked his horse with silver star spurs. He feared they had indeed ridden into a trap they'd all been too stupid to see coming.

At the Devil's Kitchen the sun struck the land with

unrelenting heat and Luther thought of a slow fire, out to roast those fool enough to try and make it across. Only men who were truly desperate would try to cross this place.

Clarence's plan was to lure Ricket out into the Kitchen. As they crossed the barren landscape Clarence intended leaving poisoned water holes behind them. His thinking was that Ricket would arrive at the Kitchen upon horses already run into the ground, whereas the animals they would be using would have been well rested and well watered. The oldster was confident he could guide safely across the Kitchen.

Right now there was no sign of Clarence. He was up on high ground, watching out for the telltale moving specks far below.

'Just looking at the place makes me feel as though I'm being sucked dry,' Luther muttered. 'I feel like a fly stuck in a spider's web.'

Miz Timberlee glared at him. 'That's fool's talk. Furthermore, I never pegged you as being of a fanciful dis-position.'

'Well, I see a place where distance is distorted. The Devil likes to play tricks upon those fool enough to walk into his kitchen. If we try to cross the salt flats we'll soon think we've headed into hell,' Luther muttered.

She laughed. 'Maybe so, but I'm a match for the devil any day.'

'Well, I reckon you are, Miz Timberlee.' Luther shrugged. 'So I guess I must keep you around, for I have found one thing worth keeping in Black Bear Crossing and it ain't Walt Grainger's spread. And the fact is, Miz Timberlee, I never want to see that two-bit town again. If you're in agreement I aim to sell Walt's spread to the first buyer I can find.'

'Well, that's fine by me, Luther. But I guess we'll take Clarence along with us. Where the hell is that crazy old coot? He had no need to back-track, because I reckon we can safely deduce there ain't anyone troubling themselves now about hunting us down.'

Donald Ricket was forced to hold his sides, for he was laughing so hard as he watched the hunting party riding for their lives. He smiled grimly. After this his reputation for being the most proficient killer on the frontier was assured. Any man who thought to disrespect him would surely think again.

The fools below still thought they were getting out of the Box with their lives. They would soon learn otherwise. He must, however, give credit where it was due. Roasting the varmints in Box Canyon had been Fernandez's idea. And a mighty fine idea it was. He shook his head. He knew damn well what Fernandez was up to now. Fernandez would be riding as though the devil were on his tail: riding to take revenge on Cooper's wife. Too bad Cooper would never know.

Flames rushed through the Canyon. Black, choking smoke filled the air. Tinder-dry shrubbery crackled as it went up. Terrified near-wild steers blindly fled the flames, crashing into everything in their path.

They crashed into the fleeing hunting party and raced on, oblivious to the screams of men and horses left in their wake.

'Ride like hell. Ride for the canyon's end. We'll get out

that away.' Digging in his spurs Cooper ignored an unseated man staggering around, clearly dazed, and another trapped beneath the bulk of a horse.

There was a scream as the waddy on foot was sent flying by a fear-crazed horse ridden by one of his fellows. No one had tried to avoid him. Now panic-filled men just rode over him.

It was every man for himself. They all understood the situation. Ricket had sprung a trap and they had ridden straight into hell. Now all they could do was hope to outrun the flames and reach the narrow exit of the canyon in time to save their hides.

From his vantage point up high Ricket watched the horror unfolding below on the floor of the canyon. He would have liked to see their features clearly as the flesh melted from their faces but he'd make do with his bird's-eye view.

The man trapped beneath the bulk of his horse screamed in terror, yelling out for someone to help him, but every last one of them ignored him. Soon he was left alone. He could scarcely breathe for the smoke, but making one last desperate effort he laboriously drew his shooter. He put one shot into the forehead of his injured horse, then pressed the barrel against his own forehead. Cursing Marcus Cooper and Donald Ricket, he squeezed the trigger.

'Damn you, Marcus Cooper. You've led us to our deaths,' a waddy screamed in terror.

Cooper would have blasted him from the saddle but this would have meant slowing the mad ride to escape.

From the canyon's high rim Ricket and his men continued to watch. They whooped with jubilation, knowing

what was in store for the fleeing riders. There was a surprise waiting for them. They'd find the narrow exit from
the box well and truly blocked.

Ricket had worked his grouching men like slaves until
they had completed the task to his satisfaction. Hell, the
fools couldn't have thought he would have left anything to
chance, could they? Well, from the way they were riding,
lashing their terrified horseflesh, they clearly had.

'Burn, you varmints, burn,' he yelled.

'Seems you've realized an honest shoot-out ain't always
the way,' Salesman, who wasn't bothering to watch the
'fun' unfolding below, observed. He paused. 'And maybe
Luther Larkin was a like-thinking man,' he concluded.

'What the hell do you mean?' Ricket did not trouble to
take his eyes away from the wall of fire sweeping through
the canyon.

'I'm saying Larkin realized he was not good enough to
beat Ollie in an honest shoot-out. The galoot simply chose
another way.' Salesman looked thoughtful. 'Hell, boss,
after we've dealt with Marcus Cooper there ain't no one
even going to recall the name of Larkin. Why put ourselves to trouble rooting out a worm when we've dealt with
one big snake. And there's no denying that when com-
pared to Cooper that two-bit rancher ain't nothing but a
worm.'

Ricket realized what Salesman was about. Barrel of lard
that the man was, he was seeking to justify forgetting all
about of Luther Larkin. Salesman, Ricket had noticed,
had not taken kindly to life on the trail.

'I'll think on what you've said.' Through pitiless eyes the
gunman watched the horror unfolding below. He relished

the cries of despair when they realized they had been out-smarted. That the exit was blocked and they were trapped. Some chose to take matters into their own hands, first shooting their horses and then themselves before flame engulfed them.

Marcus Cooper, Ricket noted with delight, actually tried desperately to climb up the canyon wall. He didn't get far before he fell back into the flames already licking at his fancy boots. As flames engulfed the man he became for a brief moment, a living torch whose screams of agony were cut short too soon.

CHAPTER 12

Of all of them Salesman feared their boss the least. So it figured that he had been elected as spokesman. Ricket's mood, he observed, had switched from downright mean to jovial.

'Well spit it out.' Ricket spoke impatiently.

'We'd all follow you to hell,' Salesman paused slightly, 'if needs be,' he concluded.

Ricket merely waited.

'Have you thought about what I said? Luther Larkin's flesh has rotted from his bones. The man is beneath notice and ain't worth the trouble of hunting down alive and especially not dead.'

'To hell with Luther Larkin!' Ricket unexpectedly grinned. 'If the varmint is still alive he can keep on running for, as you say, he ain't worth a spit.' Even as he was speaking he realized that sooner or later he'd need to rid himself of Salesman.

Salesman smiled. When this was over the law would come looking for Ricket. He'd be the one marked. The rest of them, the galoots who rode with the killer, would have plenty of chances to scatter like the tumbleweed roaming the prairie. He wiped his perspiring forehead. He'd done it. He'd turned the boss away from venturing into the Devil's Kitchen. There was no way he was going to die in that forsaken hellish place. His heart was not up to venturing out on to the salt flats. Such a place was for fools and desperate men and he was neither.

'Before we quit the territory I aim to ride out to Cooper's spread and acquaint myself with Miz Cooper,' Ricket announced.

Guffaws greeted his words.

'And nothing will give me greater pleasure than informing her that her man is now roast meat,' he concluded with a wink. 'Hell, why should Fernandez have all the fun?'

'So what the hell is going on, Clarence?' Miz Timberlee demanded as the oldster rode into camp.

'Ricket has decided his time is too valuable to be wasted on the likes of us,' Clarence muttered.

'What the hell does that mean?'

'Only that we're no-accounts, Miz Timberlee. We ain't worth troubling about. As for Cooper and crew, they were trapped in Box Canyon and burnt alive. Now Ricket has turned back. He's quitting the territory.'

Luther nodded. 'Why, I do recall the ostler telling me that years back an entire herd was driven into Box Canyon and torched way back in the old days.' He hesitated before asking, 'Now what would you do, Clarence, if you were in Ricket's boots?'

The oldster thought for a moment. 'If I were a good

deal younger and were able to put myself in Ricket's boots I would pay Black Bear Crossing a second visit. As I recall an *hombre* always got a good feeling when he was taking a town apart.'

'Why, you no-account varmint.' Seizing the coffee pot Miz Timberlee hurled it at the old man who just about managed to dodge the missile. 'We must do right and help the town!' she declared.

'Black Bear Crossing ain't our concern, Miz Timberlee,' Luther ventured.

'Hell, Luther Larkin, it is as clear as day you have never lived through being in a town being taken apart. Well I have. It ain't a pretty sight and one I would not wish on anyone.'

'Well, there ain't no need to get riled up, Miz Timberlee,' Clarence pacified. 'Because the fact is I aim to blast Donald Ricket and where better to do it than it Black Bear Crossing?'

'You care about the town, Clarence?' She sounded incredulous.

'Hell, no, Miz Timberlee, but when the day comes that I allow galoots who ain't even my equal to dismiss me as being not worth the trouble to hunt down, that's the day I'm gonna shoot myself.'

'What you're saying makes no sense.'

'I'm saying that I'm Clarence Duffy and even now I am more that a match for the likes of Donald Ricket. All I am interested in is seeing Ricket brought low. I'm heading back to that two-bit town. There is no stopping me.'

Cooper's spread appeared deserted. There were no signs

of movement. Nevertheless the riders approached warily, weapons drawn, ready to blast anything that moved.

Ricket knew he had not been wrong. He knew Fernandez had headed for this place, hell bent on vengeance.'

'Check out the bunkhouse and the barn,' he ordered. 'See if there is any sign of Fernandez's horse.'

They did not have to wait long. The man sent to check out the bunkhouse came out yelling that there were three dead inside. 'Seems they were made to kneel and then had their heads blasted off,' he supplied helpfully. 'Whoever done it got the drop on them.'

Ricket nodded. That sounded like Fernandez's work. Having no doubt once pleaded for mercy and been denied it was unlikely the man would be inclined to show mercy himself.

'No sign of Fernandez's mount,' came the yell from the barn.

Quelling his misgivings Ricket approached the ranch, Colt .45 drawn and ready. He gained entrance by simply kicking in the door and going in, Peacemaker primed to blast anything that moved. On entering the drawing room he caught his first sight of Maybelle Cooper. It was not what he wanted to see. The woman was settled in her armchair, leaning back against the cushions as though she were reclining. An ugly stain marred the front of her gown. Clear as day one single shot to the heart had ended her existence.

'Damn shame,' Ricket muttered, angry that he had been cheated out of his fun with Miz Maybelle Cooper. Why, she had been a fine-looking woman and if he had Fernandez in his sights right now he would blast the man without a qualm. No doubt, having settled an old score, the polecat had forked it out pretty damn quick.

With a sour expression on his face he came out of the ranch house. 'Seems Fernandez has done us out of our fun, for he has shot and killed Miz Cooper who was, I'd say, a mighty fine-looking woman.' As he had expected, a volley of insults erupted, all of them aimed at Fernandez.

Salesman stayed silent. Fernandez was the only one of them with any sense. He'd taken his revenge and then forked it out pretty damn quick. Salesman would have liked to fork it out himself but he knew darn well that that crazy son of a bitch Donald Ricket would very likely blast him out of the saddle.

'Black Bear Crossing it is,' Ricket announced. 'We'll hit the town tomorrow.' He glanced at the darkening sky. 'I guess we must avail ourselves of Cooper's hospitality. Let's see what he's got to drink. Not rot-gut liquor, I'm sure. Only the best would have done for the likes of him. And get Miz Cooper wrapped in a blanket and hauled out to the bunkhouse. We'll burn the place together with the ranch house when we leave tomorrow.'

'They'll be as drunk as skunks tomorrow,' Salesman warned. 'The varmints won't be able to walk steady, let alone see straight.'

'They'll sober up soon enough and they'll be ready to ride when I say so. Now it ain't possible to rein them in for they're going to take Cooper's ranch apart and discover every bottle he has got stowed away. All you've got to do tomorrow is brew coffee. Plenty of it! They might not know it but the folk in Black Bear Crossing are waiting on our arrival and we ain't about to let them down.'

*

Luther shivered. Early morning was damn cold. He waited while the greyness of breaking dawn gave way to the light of day. He found that he had not rejoiced that Cooper had been turned into roast meat, for many others, men and horses, had perished alongside Marcus Cooper.

Why in tarnation, he wondered, would Miz Timberlee decide that now was a time to do right and that it had fallen to them to save the two-bit town from the terror of Donald Ricket? Personally he didn't give a damn about the town. He wasn't fooling himself. He was here for Miz Timberlee and nothing else, whereas Clarence, crazy old coot that he had become, was simply here because he had allowed a fool idea into his head.

'We'll take the upward trail,' Clarence declared, 'and maybe, just maybe, we might get to town before Donald Ricket. If I were in his boots and had heard about Cooper's fine-looking wife, why I might have been tempted to pay her a call.'

'Then maybe we should—'

'No. Either way it is too late to help her. We must first head for town.'

As they rode along the canyon's rim Luther resolved not to look down into the canyon's floor. He had no wish to see whatever pitiful remains of men and horseflesh might be revealed.

Was it too much to hope that Ricket might have decided to let the town be? He guessed it was.

*

'If you think you can come back to town, well, you are mistaken. My husband for one never believed Walt Grainger's confession.' Mrs Collins sniffed. 'You will not escape again. The men hereabouts will have something to say about that!'

'Oh, will they indeed!' Miz Timberlee spoke up. 'Are you including Mr Collins amongst the men?'

'Well naturally I am.'

Miz Timberlee smiled. 'Well, I am sorry to say your husband's days of saying anything about anything are over.' She paused slightly. 'Your husband, along with the rest of Cooper's hunting party, was burnt to a crisp in Box Canyon. Donald Ricket outsmarted the lot of them. I guess it was not hard to do.'

'That's a lie! But you're good at lying! We all know that!'

'I'm afraid she ain't, ma'am,' Luther spoke up. Clearly the woman had come from town. And that meant that Donald Ricket had not yet hit the town.

So where the hell was he? Had the varmint gone after Maybelle Cooper? He had to remind himself that she had been the one to send Arthur Blunt to whip him to shreds. Even so, his every instinct was to head for Cooper's spread. Wisely, upon seeing Miz Timberlee's expression, he kept quiet.

'And there's more,' he continued. 'We believe Donald Ricket will be headed back to Black Bear Crossing mighty soon.'

'Which means we ought to get moving.' Clarence urged his horse forward. As they moved away Mrs Collins began screaming hysterically that it was all lies.

'Damn fool woman,' Clarence muttered. 'Best be prepared for trouble when we arrive in town, and I am telling you now, any fool takes a shot at me, well, he's gonna lose his head.' His expression was grim and brooked no opposition.

'You must be crazy, coming back to our town, Luther Larkin!' The speaker was the town barber. Luther recalled that the fellow had been on the jury that had found him guilty of murdering Hamish Cooper.

The barber waved his shotgun threateningly. Kenna had told them what had occurred last time when Ricket had ridden in. There had been no one waving shotguns then.

'We've no time to waste. Donald Ricket is about to hit town.' Luther paused. 'Again,' he concluded.

'You damn liar. Ricket is running for his life, pursued by Marcus Cooper.'

'No, he ain't. Marcus Cooper is dead, roasted like the rest of them in Box Canyon. Seems like they rode right into Ricket's trap,' Luther explained.

'You're a damn liar,' the barber reiterated, as though trying to convince himself that this could not be. He levelled his rifle. 'You lied about not killing Hamish Cooper and you are lying now.'

'Put that rifle down, you damn fool.' Kenna walked on to Main Street. In his hand was a Colt .45. This was surprising, for the man had not been known to carry a gun.

'You won't shoot me, Kenna. You ain't got the nerve, besides which you've got to live in this town once this is over.'

'I guess I have.' Kenna nodded his agreement and

lowered the muzzle of his .45.

The barber smirked, but not for long, as Kenna without warning discharged his .45. His slug thudded into the barber's booted foot. Howling, the man dropped his shotgun, all thoughts of blasting Luther driven out of his head by the agony in his foot.

'You no-account bum.' Clarence regarded with contempt the man as he rolled around on the ground, clutching a foot. For a moment there Luther thought the oldster was actually going to shoot the galoot.

'Now you folk listen good,' Luther yelled. 'Donald Ricket is headed back to town. You ain't seen the last of the man. This time it's gonna be far worse!' If Ricket did not return to town hell, what a fool he would appear!

'Why, the man will have the whole territory up in arms.' Reverend Dent put in an appearance. 'Why would he come back here?'

Clarence spat. The gob landed on Dent's boot. 'Because the polecat cannot help himself,' he declared with conviction. 'No more than you men could help turning yellow last time Ricket rode into town.' He laughed. 'Sure as hell the devil is whispering in Ricket's ear. "Why not have some fun?" he is saying.'

'We've got to get organized,' Luther ploughed on. 'We need men on rooftops. What we've got to do is block him in once he hits Main Street.'

'Surely it makes more sense to get out of town?'

'Do you think he'll let anyone leave without running them down?' Luther argued. 'Just you folk remember how Marcus Cooper met his end.'

'We've only your word for that, Luther Larkin.'

'Hell, what mangy curs you men are,' Luther declared.

'Well, I'm with you,' Kenna declared. 'And so is under-taker Crisp by the look of things although he cannot tell you himself, for he lost the ability to speak when Ricket hung him high. The fact is he would be dead right now if a kid had not blasted the hanging rope. Yep, young Tommy Kelly sure put the rest of the men in this town to shame.'

'Just tell us what you want us to do.' Dent capitulated. 'After all, the good book says an eye for an eye, which makes dealing with Donald Ricket entirely justified.'

With tears streaming down her cheeks Mrs Collins took up the reins and headed for home. When she spotted the bunched riders approaching from an eastern angle, for the briefest moment she hoped her husband was safe. And then, realizing otherwise, screaming she frantically whipped her horses.

Donald Ricket eyed the careering buggy, which he saw was being driven by a woman of middling years and expanded girth. He grinned.

'Let's see how far she can get before we get her.'

Firing their weapons in the air, none of the men had any intention to shoot her, they set off in pursuit. All save one.

Salesman frowned. Ricket, it seemed was too easily diverted these days from planned objectives. *Hit the town and get out fast* was the plan for, after all, their window of opportunity was small. News of the outrage would circulate quickly enough. Fortunately the telegraph had not yet arrived in Black Bear Crossing. Had it been there an army of men would be out hunting them down.

He made a quick decision. To hell with the lot of them! He had always known when to ride away. He crossed the trail and continued on his way. He rode west, away from the town of Black Bear Crossing.

Ricket chose to prolong the woman's torment by allowing her to believe that she was getting away. He had his men drop back, allowed the distance between them to lengthen, then surged forward until he got tired of playing cat and mouse. 'Let's get her!' He dug in his spurs.

Mrs Collins, mad with terror, still lashing her sweat-drenched horses, never saw what was coming her way as her buggy wheel hit a rock, causing the buggy to flip over bringing down the horses and throwing Mrs Collins clear.

'Hell!' Ricket declared as he reined in his horse. 'Fool woman has gone and broke her neck.' He laughed. 'Too bad for us, then! Best put the horses out of their misery.'

Salesman heard the sound of distant shots. He guessed the buggy had gone over and the horses were being shot. As for the woman, if she was alive, well she would delay Ricket and the men. If she were not, well, that did not matter, for Ricket's hands were tied. Fired up, the men's only thoughts would be to get to Black Bear Crossing damn quick.

Taking a town apart was addictive, like taking a smoke.

Ricket eyed the town of Black Bear Crossing. Life seemed normal enough in the town. Men were strolling around, although few females could be seen. This was not surprising considering what had happened when he'd last visited this town.

He never would have thought Salesman would have

chickened out at the last moment. He'd been all for running Salesman down but the expressions worn by his crew had told him otherwise. Fired up, they could only think of hitting the town. So for now his hands were tied with regards to Salesman.

He took a deep breath. 'We ride out this evening and we keep going until we are out of the territory. I don't give a damn what any man gets up to as long as that man can sit the saddle at the appointed time. And I am telling you now that I aim to blast anyone who ain't capable of hauling himself into the saddle. That's fair enough, I say. Does anyone disagree?'

No one did.

'Let's not keep Black Bear Crossing waiting.' He drew his shooter.

As they thundered into town the folk on Main Street scattered for cover like so many scared rabbits.

From the livery barn the ostler watched as Donald Ricket thundered past, clearly headed for the saloon. In times such as this liquor always came before women. Mercifully the town had decided to believe Luther Larkin. They were prepared and had found the guts to fight.

As Ricket arrived mid-street, a shot rang out but missed its target, Ricket himself, as the shooter was trembling far too much to be able to shoot straight.

'What the hell,' the gunman bellowed, momentarily unable to accept the truth that a no-account bum had taken a pot shot at him.

As more shots rang out his men returned fire and a man plunged down from the roof. Realization dawned: they'd ridden into an ambush.

'Fork it out! Fork it out!' Ricket bellowed. He'd burn the whole damn town to the ground for this.

As gunfire erupted on Main Street the men waiting in terror behind the livery barn frantically pushed two wagons loaded with hay on to Main Street. Miz Timberlee, Mrs Kelly and Reverend Dent lit their torches and rushed out to set the kerosene-soaked hay on fire.

'Goddamnit!' A string of profanities spilled from Ricket's lips as they were confronted by a wall of fire. Jerking his horse round viciously he rode back along Main Street to find that way out of town also blocked, although in this case the wagons had merely been overturned. But they still had a chance, he reckoned, for their ambushers were in no way fighting men, just two-bit townsfolk who'd somehow found the guts to put up a fight.

Luther waited with Clarence inside the saloon. The oldster was as obstinate as an old mule.

'I want Ricket to see my face when I blast him!' he declared. Personally Luther could not see it mattered a damn when it came to seeing the face of the *hombre* who had fired the fatal slug. But Clarence thought otherwise and was, moreover, convinced that Ricket would seek refuge in the saloon. Now as he listened to the yells and curses from outside, standing shoulder to shoulder with a crazy old coot who clearly had a death wish, Luther regretted again that Miz Timberlee had taken it into her head to do right.

'They ain't up to the job,' Clarence cackled, referring to the shooters outside. 'Any time now, any time now.' He sounded damned pleased with the prospect of a shoot-out.

Luther nodded. He knew the town was running scared.

For himself he felt detached from it all. He guessed that was what the state penitentiary did to a man.

'Get inside,' Ricket bellowed, for the damn varmints were going for the bigger target now – the horses. The saloon offered a degree of cover. 'We ain't done for. We'll fight our way out!'

As the desperate killers burst through the batwings Luther and Clarence triggered their shooters. Men went down screaming and Ricket had scarcely time to realize he'd led his men into a second trap before a bullet struck him in the chest. He went down, knowing he was done for.

Clarence came out from behind the bar and stood over the man he had downed.

'I'm Clarence Duffy,' he announced. 'The Donald Ricket of my day.'

Ricket spoke with difficulty. 'Well, I ain't never heard of you.' The light left his eyes before the old man could think of a retort.

Outside someone was screaming that Mrs Standish had gone crazy and was attacking the killers who had fallen on Main Street with an axe, while Miz Timberlee was heard yelling 'Just let her be until she wears herself out.'

The new lawman rode into town. He'd heard plenty about this town, none of it good. Men had been chopped into pieces in this town. Townsfolk had shut up like clams when outsiders had asked questions.

He recognized the man loading supplies into a wagon.

'Well, if it ain't Luther Larkin from the state penitentiary.' He paused. 'Warden Comfrey has turned up, pieces of him at least. I guess your old pard Ambrose Penrose has been busy. Got anything to say?'

The woman sitting in the wagon spoke up.

'We don't talk about those times do we, Mr Larkin!'

Luther Larkin, who had been about to tell the lawman to go to hell and that Comfrey had deserved what he had got, reconsidered.

'That we don't, Mrs Larkin,' he agreed.

'Good day to you then, lawman!' She glared at the new arrival.

The lawman rode on. Clear as day Larkin was a damn fool. He'd been given his freedom and then some could say he'd thrown it away!